Tony
O'GALLAGHER

Clanwe Yashpack

novum pro

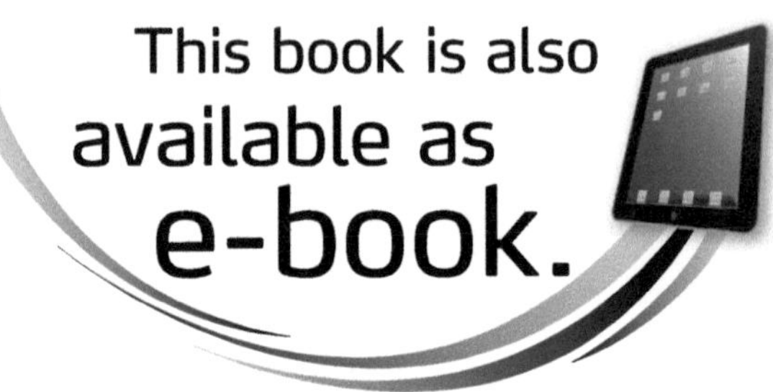

www.novum-publishing.co.uk

© 2024 novum publishing

ISBN 978-3-99146-346-7
Editing: Samantha Acker
Cover photos: Sebastian Sikora, Ruslan Galiullin | Dreamstime.com
Cover design, layout & typesetting: novum publishing

www.novum-publishing.co.uk

Inhaltsverzeichnis

Prologue

I am 214 years old, although people tell me I have the appearance of a man in his sixties. Understandably, I have frequently been asked about the reasons for my longevity. After all, I am more than 80 years older than any other human being on the planet. Usually, I try to avoid answering the question directly. Often, I explain why I do not think genetics play any great part. I point out that my father died at age 59. My mother was just 70, and two of my grandparents died before they reached 60. My children and grandchildren have all predeceased me with none of them reaching 85 years of age. Just one of my great grandchildren is still alive having reached 92 years of age. If pressed, I waffled on about eating a healthy diet, getting plenty of exercise and drinking the occasional glass of red wine. The healthy diet and exercise are essentially true, but the bit about the red wine is very much an understatement.

The real reason for my longevity is well-known to me but, until now, I have been unwilling to divulge it for two reasons. Firstly, it was always most probable that people would not believe me and would dismiss me as either a fantasist or as someone suffering from senile dementia. Secondly, I was afraid of the consequences for some very good friends of mine. But circumstances have changed, and I am now prepared to tell all.

Strange as it may seem, the whole matter has its origins in my not possessing a television. Following a relationship breakdown, I moved into rented accommodation where I lived alone. Before this, I had watched very little television other than news or sports. So, I made the decision not to have a television. In due course, that led to the receipt of a letter each month from the television licensing people threatening dire consequences if I was found to be watching or downloading programmes without a licence. These I ignored because, even if I were to inform them that I did not have a television, they would come to check anyway.

I still watch television occasionally. If I wished to watch a particular sporting event, I watched it in the pub. So, it was then when I happened to be in the Phoenix in the evening that it all began.

Liverpool was playing in the Champions League that evening. During half-time, a chap called Billy McConkey arrived at the bar. Billy described himself as a businessman, and he certainly was involved in various ventures. Whether all of these ventures were legitimate was very much open to question.

Whatever about his business activities, Billy's generosity was never called into question. By all accounts, he paid his employees well, and he was known to buy rounds of drinks for the entire bar.

Billy enquired if anyone knew of a water diviner. He explained that he had purchased a plot of land on which he intended to build a home. He had been informed that an underground stream was suspected to be running through the plot, and he wanted to track its course so that he would not receive any nasty surprises whenever the foundations were excavated. There was also the possibility of sinking a well or using the stream to feed a pond or small lake. Billy's enquiry provoked much discussion. Some of the bar regulars expressed great scepticism regarding water divining. Others said they had an open mind on the subject. None of them knew of any water diviners. All were amazed when I stated that I could divine water.

Billy asked if I would undertake the work stating that he would pay well. When asked, he said the plot was just over three acres. I told him that surveying a plot of that size would take quite some time and was just about to suggest a fee of £300 when Billy offered a fee of £500. We agreed to meet at 9.30 the next morning so that Billy could take me to the land in question. When he asked if there was anything he would need to bring, I told him I would need a couple of cans of spray paint of any colour except green.

Chapter 1

Billy gave me a quizzical glance when I climbed into his SUV. In addition to a rucksack containing a packed lunch, I was carrying two wire coat hangers which I had straightened out into straight rods. He had been expecting me to have a forked piece of hazel. His questions kept coming. How did I learn to divine water? Why did I have metal rods? Was I a seventh son of a seventh son?

My answers surprised him. For the first 63 years of my life, I had been blissfully unaware of my ability. It so happened that the installation of a water metre at a friend Brigid's house in County Louth indicated that there was leakage in the system within the bounds of the one-acre property. Brigid had brought in Johnny, who is a water diviner, to trace the route of the connection to the mains. This he did using two straightened wire coat hangers. He held them loosely by their ends around waist height, parallel to each other pointing straight in front of him as he walked slowly. When he came over the water pipe, the rods swung so that they crossed each other and pointed downwards.

After Johnny had left, I took the rods and, out of curiosity, imitated what he had done. To my amazement, I got the same reaction from the rods, although others who tried did not. I still do not know how the rods work or why only a small minority of people can divine water.

Billy's plot was in an idyllic location. It was gently sloping and overlooked a broad valley. Behind part of it rose a high steep hill whilst the rest was in front of a col between that hill and a lower neighbour. The view from in front of the col was breathtaking, and it was there on that side of the plot Billy wished to build. He marked the circumference of his proposed house which, in my estimation, covered just over 4,500 square feet. "So, it is not going to be a small bungalow?" I asked. "Who said anything about a bungalow?" replied Billy. "If it is two storeys, it will be some house," I remarked. "Not two," he said. "Three, or, more accurately, four, if you count the garage and wine cellar, I will have under part of it." It emerged that he intended to have two full storeys and a third extending to around half the width of the lower two with a roof terrace occupying the other half.

Such a building, however well designed, was most unlikely to comply with planning regulations, but Billy was confident he would obtain planning permission. Aware of Billy's shady reputation, I referred to brown envelopes. He laughed and said, "Suppose, just suppose, a hypothetical situation exists. Suppose a Chief Planning Officer has a gambling problem. He has an account with a bookmaker who has permitted him to run up a debt of enormous proportions. He is way out of his depth. Now, suppose that bookmaker submits a planning application. Can you really see it being refused?"

The picture was now clear. Billy had a majority stake in Winbig, a local chain of bookmakers. His behaviour, whilst not actually illegal, stank to high heaven. Still, it was none of my business. Whilst I was not happy about going along with such activity, there was probably nothing to be gained by backing out of our arrangement. The thought occurred to me that I could expose the situation to the authorities or the media. But, aside from not relishing making enemies of Billy and his associates, it was quite possible that all I would achieve was to make a fool of myself. Billy probably had yet to submit the application. After all, the application would need to specify the precise location of the planned dwelling, and Billy was using my services to avoid picking a location affected by the underground stream. Besides, he could probably find some other water diviner or even use a few test boreholes. I would just have to hold my nose and do what I had agreed to do.

So, I told Billy I would start by checking the proposed site of the house and then cover the rest of the land. Although no expert, I did not expect the stream to interfere with the site, but I did not tell Billy this lest he decide that he no longer needed my services. Just as I was starting, Billy received a call on his mobile. After a brief cryptic conversation, he informed me he had to head off to sort out a problem, but he should be back within an hour or so. Off he went. I was aware that the "or so" could well prove to be longer than the hour but I was not concerned. It was a beautiful spring morning. I had my lunch with me and, if needs be, I could walk home in a little more than an hour.

Walking slowly up and down with the rods was quite relaxing. Each time I turned, I shifted about two feet across the site. I had already formed the view that it was most unlikely I would find the stream in this part of the plot, but it was safest to make certain. Even if I found a stream elsewhere in the plot, that would not be a guarantee that a second stream, either a tributary or fully separate from the first, did not exist. So back and forth I walked until my rods suddenly jerked upright so that they were vertical and became very warm, almost hot.

That really surprised me. It was something I had never previously experienced. So, I took a couple of steps backwards and walked forward again. The same thing happened. I tried to move forward, but the rods seemed to be against a solid barrier. I tried walking forward holding the rods hanging loosely at either side of me but again they swung upwards. Setting the rods on the ground, I had no problem walking forward.

After marking the spot, further attempts to walk on parallel tracks revealed that the barrier followed a straight line that intersected with one proposed side wall about halfway along and with the proposed back wall about one-third of the way along. I wondered what I would find if I approached the barrier from the other side and discovered I could take the rods through, provided I carried them in one hand. When I approached from several feet away from the first barrier, a second one revealed its presence running parallel to the first about five feet away from it. Curiously, if I approached from less than five feet away, the first barrier did not seem to exist.

If one looked along the direction of the barriers, one would be looking through the col, so up I went and surveyed the next valley. It was then that a realisation dawned on me. On the far side of the valley was Knocknashee – the hill of the fairies. That is where there is a reputed fairy fort. There is not much to see other than an old hawthorn tree standing in the centre of a circle of standing stones, which is about forty feet in diameter. Despite its description as a fairy fort, I had never heard about any tales of reputed fairy activity at the spot.

But what, if anything, lies in the other direction? Trusting that Billy would not return too quickly, I set off in the other direction. I had not gone more than a quarter mile when I came across an old hawthorn tree standing in the middle of a field. Almost certainly, any local would tell me it was a fairy thorn.

I recalled as a child hearing stories about a house that had experienced problems because it was built straddling the route between two fairy thorns, or so the story had gone. Could a similar fate befall Billy's planned creation? The thought caused a shiver to run up my spine. It is a brave, perhaps foolhardy, man who will interfere with any fairy thorn or the route between the two of them. Legend has it that the fairies tend to exact revenge. I was not the one who was going to build across the route or live in the house, but I was associated with the project. Billy must be persuaded to move the site of the house.

That might prove easier said than done. For a start, Billy **definitely** did not believe in fairies. One night in the Phoenix, the talk had been about ghosts. Billy had been quite vehement in dismissing the possibility of their existence. "Ghosts, vampires, werewolves, poltergeists, fairies, leprechauns! All a load of total shite!" had been his contribution to the discussion. Worse still, persuading Billy that a fairy pathway crossed the property would in no way help the situation. Billy's instinct would be to try and profit from the situation by turning the fairy road into a visitor attraction. If Cooley could profit from leprechauns, then Billy could profit from fairies. That could well bring down the fairies' wrath on all concerned.

While walking back to Billy's land, it occurred to me that the solution might lie in persuading him that there existed some other problem within the site. So, I erased as best I could the marks outlining the fairy road and then drew a circle with a diameter of around fifteen feet towards the other end of the house. This was going to be where the "problem" lay.

Locating the underground stream proved straightforward. It was pretty much where I expected it to be. It was also sufficiently far away from his planned site to allow a fresh site to be used between the stream and the original site, thus avoiding any interference with the fairy road.

Billy arrived back just as I was finishing marking the route of the stream. His initial reaction was one of delight because the stream would not interfere with his site. He was much less pleased when I drew his attention to the "problem" ground. My story was that I was finding a strange reaction by the rods over that area. It was a lot weaker than that from the stream, and I really did not know what the cause was. All I could offer by way of explanation was, of necessity, speculation. One possibility was an underground deposit of a metallic ore with magnetic properties. This would not cause any problems with the construction of the house but who knows what effect it might have on electronic equipment. Many items, including computers, televisions, game consoles, alarms and security cameras were likely to be affected. Another possible explanation was that there was soft or swampy ground beneath the surface that could cause problems with construction.

I told Billy I would like to investigate the matter further. If I could replicate the rods' reaction, that should give me a good idea as to what the problem was. Firstly, I would like to try the rods over different pieces of soft or swampy ground. One area where there was a large area where the ground varied from just a little soft to very swampy was the great bog beside the Newry-Portadown canal. The other theory might prove more difficult to investigate, but I thought I should be able to set up experiments with magnets of various strengths. I did not tell Billy that I was already aware that power lines, whether overhead or buried, elicited a strong reaction from the rods. I wanted him to believe that swampy ground was the cause of the "problem."

The nonsense about a magnetic deposit was designed to muddy the waters. By way of demonstration, I faked a weak reaction over the ground within the circle and then showed him a much stronger reaction over the stream. I had a moment of panic when Billy asked if he could try using the rods to see whether or not he could divine water. I could not very well refuse and so I was distinctly relieved when Billy got no reaction from the rods over the stream. Had he done so, the lack of any reaction over the ground within the circle would have occasioned me major difficulty.

Billy really did not want to move his site. It afforded a better view than anywhere else on the plot. He took the line that neither possible cause presented an insurmountable problem. If it was swampy ground, then the site could be piled if necessary. If it was some sort of magnetic deposit, then the foundation and subfloor could incorporate some sort of Faraday cage that would eliminate the problem. He reckoned that it need not involve much more than incorporating steel mesh reinforcing into the founds and subfloors. He added that, even without a Faraday cage, only a small portion of the site was affected, leaving plenty of room for electronic equipment within the rest of the house. There was no effective argument I could deploy to convince him the site needed to be moved. Additional expenses did not appear to present any problem. I was also aware that if I tried too hard to persuade him to move the site, it could well arouse suspicion. Once I had made him aware of a potential problem, how he handled it was up to him.

Having handed to me twenty-five twenties, Billy dropped me home. That night, I found sleep very elusive as I tried to come up with some solution to the situation in which I found myself. The £500 which had first appeared to be easy money now seemed poor compensation for my present trouble.

Chapter 2

In the days that followed, I tried to push the matter to the back of my mind. If I was going to fall foul of the fairies, there was nothing I could do to prevent it. But my thoughts kept returning to the subject that led me to researching the evidence for the existence or otherwise of fairies, especially at Knocknashee.

My efforts brought me into contact with Ciaran Donnelly, a local historian who had given a talk on fairy folklore a couple of years previously. He was quite delighted at my interest in the subject and invited me to his house one evening. He had little useful information to offer regarding the fairy fort at Knocknashee. Yes, he could find references to the fairy fort in old records and documents dating back centuries, but that, in itself, meant very little. The name, Knocknashee, is a corruption of the Gaelic *Cnoc na Sí*, meaning hill of the fairies, commentators could well have referred to a fairy fort without any other evidence whatsoever. Certainly, references to fairy activity in the area are fewer to the extent of being nonexistent. Ciaran told me I might have had more success if I had started my enquiries a couple of years earlier and proceeded to recount what he knew about Mickey McAteer.

He had first heard about Mickey from his Uncle Alec who, like other locals, regarded Mickey with more than a little curiosity. On first impression, Mickey was a typical bachelor farmer with a cottage and around forty acres. He did not farm the land himself. Instead, he let all the land on conacre. He claimed to be the last of his line, which could very well have been true. Nobody in the locality had any memory of Mickey's parents or of any siblings of his. Stranger still, nobody had any memory of Mickey as anything other than a middle-aged man. Alec had told Ciaran of walking to primary school and seeing Mickey leaning over a five-barred gate smoking his pipe. He looked the same then as he did when Alec started drawing the old age pension.

Mickey mostly kept to himself. Indeed, he would not be seen around the locality for weeks at a time, even months. Even on the rare occasion when he visited McGeough's Pub, there was little conversation to be had with Mickey. He sat in a corner, and his replies to any attempts to start a conversation with him tended to be monosyllabic. The locals regarded him as an eccentric old boy and, while they harboured a great deal of curiosity about him, for the most part, left him alone. However, one night, Mickey consumed more than his normal quota of drinks and became quite intoxicated. In his drunken state, he told the assembled company that he was friends with the fairies, had visited them and that he could speak a little of their language. He uttered a few phrases which, for all his listeners knew, could have been Swahili, Double Dutch or just plain gibberish. Most of those present watched and listened with mild amusement, but a couple of them started to take a handout of Mickey by coming out with their own pieces of gibberish, claiming to speak Leprechaunese.

At this, Mickey became ferociously angry, roaring at them that the fairies would punish their insulting behaviour. He cursed them roundly and stormed out of the pub. There followed his longest absence from the locality of around three and a half years.

Ciaran said that he had been fascinated when he heard all this from his uncle and had resolved to interview Mickey as part of a project on folklore on which he was then engaged. However, the interview proved difficult to arrange because Mickey seemed to spend more time away from the cottage than he did living in it. On numerous occasions, he had called to find the cottage deserted. Eventually, he heard that Mickey had been seen a couple of days earlier and, approaching the cottage, saw smoke coming from the chimney.

When he knocked on the door, he was surprised when it was answered by a woman. She explained that she lived a couple of hundred yards down the road. She had seen Mickey the previous day, and he seemed quite unwell. Overnight, he had become worse and was suffering from a very high fever. The doctor had

been there and wanted Mickey to go to hospital but he had refused. He had nobody else to look after him, and she was being a good Samaritan, trying her best to tend to him and make
him comfortable. But he seemed to be getting worse and was
now delirious. She asked Ciaran if he would be kind enough to
sit with Mickey for an hour. She needed to go home to get a few
things done, including feeding the chickens.

Ciaran agreed as it would have been heartless not to. As he sat
by the bed, he listened to the ravings of the man lying in it. But as
he listened, he gradually realised that the ravings were remarkably lucid. He heard a detailed description of what Mickey had
seen as he watched King William and his army pass by heading
southwards. Having studied the Williamite campaign in Ireland,
Ciaran was struck by how closely Mickey's description tallied
with what he knew. It was quite amazing that this man knew
so much about William's army. Then the narrative switched,
and Mickey recounted details of a spell spent working on the
canal from Portadown-Newry. This had been built during the
1730s, and, again, Mickey's account accorded with the very detailed research Ciaran had conducted into the relevant historical documents. Ciaran was well acquainted with all historians
in Northern Ireland and had never come across Mickey in historical circles. So how did this man know so much?

Whilst he was pondering this, Mickey opened his eyes and
stared at Ciaran. His talk seemed to become incoherent, but a certain phrase seemed to recur. It sounded like *clanwe yashpak*. After
a while, the talking stopped, and he seemed to drift into sleep.

In due course, Ciaran heard the neighbour re-entering the
cottage. As he was rising from the chair, he noticed a yellowing
scrap of newspaper on the bedside table. Written on it in pen-
cil were two lines. One was *clanwe yashpak*, and the other read:
"Always strive for the greater good." Wishing to investigate this
strange language and, thinking he was doing no harm, he took
the scrap of paper with him as he left the cottage.

The following morning, he received a phone call from the
neighbour informing him that Mickey had passed away in the

early hours. She said that it was likely that his neighbours would come together to organise his funeral, and Ciaran asked that he be informed of the arrangements once they were known. A few days later, he had attended one of the more unusual funerals he had witnessed. No family was present, and nobody had any idea of the age of the deceased.

Ciaran's research into the strange language had proved fruitless. He had contacted the language department of several universities but not only did nobody know the language, but nobody could even hazard a guess as to what it might be.

The scrap of newspaper had been more informative but just as puzzling. Extensive research had finally revealed that it came from a copy of the Belfast Newsletter dated 4 October 1794. How had Mickey come by a piece of newspaper over 200 years old? Its possession would normally suggest that Mickey had been some sort of historian, but Ciaran was unaware of any such activity on Mickey's part. Add in that no historian would ever dream of writing on such an artefact. On the other hand, his detailed and accurate knowledge of William's army and work on the canal in the eighteenth century must have come from somewhere. It was all a bit of a mystery.

I asked if Ciaran had been able to establish just what age Mickey had been. Ciaran stated he had spent considerable time researching this question. He had visited the Registrar's Office at Stranmillis University College and pulled a few strings to obtain direct access to the register. His uncle had known Mickey for at least sixty years, so he could not have been born later than 1950 and, given that Alec remembered Mickey as a middle-aged man in the late 1950s, it seemed likely that Mickey had been born sometime around 1900. Nevertheless, Ciaran searched the records from 1922 to 1955. Finding nothing, he headed to Dublin to the search facility at the Irish Life Centre and searched backwards from 1922 to the earliest available records. Again, he found nothing. Unsurprisingly, there were several entries in each jurisdiction for Michael McAteer, but none of them appeared to be the right person. With all of them, he had been able to check the baptismal records in the local Catholic church. Such records are always noted with details of any marriage in a Catholic church anywhere in the world. Each Michael McAteer had been married.

It was certainly not impossible that Mickey, unbeknownst to his neighbours, had married but, whether or not he had, he was becoming a real mystery man. I speculated on the possibility that he had been born somewhere in Great Britain or even overseas. I had searched in vain for any record of my paternal grandmother's birth both in Ireland and Scotland. There was a possibility that she had been born on the family tea plantation in India. Could something similar explain the lack of records for Mickey?

But, if he had been born elsewhere, how did he come by his farm? Ciaran had checked with Land Registry and there existed no record of him purchasing it so it would seem to have been inherited.

Ciaran and I chatted late into the night over a couple of glasses of single malt. I casually enquired as to the existence of any other fairy forts in the locality. He stated that there was nothing other than a few fairy thorn trees. He did not mention any fairy highways, so I reckoned the was no local knowledge of what I had found.

The following day was spent trying to make some sort of sense out of the things Ciaran had told me. Several questions bugged me. Why did nobody have any memory of Mickey's parents? Why did Alec remember him from his schooldays as a middle-aged man when he still looked like a middle-aged man over sixty years later? Why was there no record of Mickey's birth? What was Mickey doing with a small scrap of a newspaper from over two hundred years ago? Did the strange words have any meaning, or were they just part of the ravings of a delusional man?

It was difficult to construct a coherent answer. The best I could come up with was that Mickey's birth had simply not been registered. Such things were not completely unknown. He was only around forty years old when Alec was at school, leaving him to be just over a hundred years old when he died. His parents had died when he was in his mid-teens, meaning that one would need to be in one's mid-nineties to have any possible memory of them.

It was not great. I was aware that it stretched what was possible to the limit, and I would not have liked to have to convince anybody it was the right answer, but the other possibilities were worse. That a whole townland had suffered collective amnesia? That Mickey had been over 125 years old? One positive feature of my theory was that it might be possible to establish that, at least, part of it was correct. Counting back from 2017, Mickey would have been born circa 1912. A search of death records for the period between then and 1930, or even as far as 1935, might well establish that he was orphaned at an early age. It then struck me that there might be another angle of approach. The census records for 1911 should show who was living in the farm cottage at the time.

A phone call to Ciaran revealed he had not checked census records. He had simply been curious about Mickey's age, and, having started with birth registers, just kept going. I also enquired if he had checked for any grave for Mickey's parents. He replied that he had. Mickey had been buried in a new grave since there was no record of any grave of any relatives of his. There is a McAteer family plot in the cemetery, but they are a quite separate family.

This information made me rethink my plans. The parents had not been buried in the local cemetery, and I had no way of discovering where they had been buried. Their Christian names were unknown, so any search would be pointless. This left the census records, which were easily checked online. In 1911, the only person recorded as living in the cottage was a Michael Christopher McAteer. Similarly, in 1901, only Michael Christopher McAteer was in residence. This simply could not be Mickey! The earliest age at which he could possibly have been living there alone was twelve, and that was stretching credulity. This would mean that he was born no later than 1889, putting him at 128 or older when he died. This was impossible to reconcile with him looking like a man in his sixties when he died. The only explanation that I could think of was that Mickey's father had been widowed before 1901 or had maybe never married. Shortly after 1911, he fathered an illegitimate child whose birth was registered using the mother's surname. His father died when Mickey was around twelve or thirteen, and then Mickey took over the farm whilst adopting McAteer as his surname. His mother died shortly afterwards and was buried in her family plot.

I was happy with this theory until, just as I was dozing off in bed that night, the question of his father's grave, or absence thereof, reared its head again. Where was he buried? The awful thought came to my mind that Mickey had resented his father. Illegitimacy carried quite a stigma in those times. Or perhaps his father mistreated his mother. Perhaps the resentment was sufficiently strong to drive Mickey, once he had acquired the physical strength, to murder his father and bury him somewhere on the farm.

Once again, I had a theory based on improbabilities and, this time, no realistic prospect of testing it. I might be able to divine water, but I doubted whether my rods would be of any use in detecting buried human remains which, by now, would consist of just bones and teeth. If I were to suggest to the authorities that they excavate up to forty acres, my sanity would certainly be called into question.

Mickey would just have to remain a mystery.

Chapter 3

Life settled back into its normal routine until, three weeks later, I was accosted in the street by Billy. "What sort of a complete eejit are you anyway?" he demanded. "I paid good money for a guy to sink a few boreholes in that circle you drew. But if you go down about fifteen feet, you meet solid rock. Soft ground, my arse! I also got him to check the area with a magnetometer. It didn't register the slightest flicker. Did you think I came up the Clanrye in a bubble? All that is saving you from me handing you his invoice is that he found the stream exactly where you marked it."

I tried to explain that all I had said was that I had gotten a weak reaction with the rods, but Billy was not interested. So, as far as he was concerned, some fanciful notions of mine had cost him money, and he was not best pleased. I had to admit to myself that he was much closer to the truth than he could possibly realise. Even though I had acted with the best of intentions, I did not like the fact that I had cost Billy money.

The encounter unsettled me. Was this fairy highway going to continue to haunt me? I decided that I might as well discover as much as possible about the feature. At present, it was only an assumption that it ran from the fairy fort to the fairy thorn trees. It needed to be mapped for its entire length.

But I needed to be careful how I went about the task. I could not mark the route on the ground. If Billy, or anyone he had hired to do any work at the site, spotted any marks, their suspicions could be aroused. I would be a prime suspect and what explanation could I possibly offer? So, off I went to Waterstones and had them order in the relevant Ordnance Survey map in the six-inches-to-a-mile series.

So, I arrived at the fairy thorn trees one morning carrying a packed lunch, the map, my divining rods and a borrowed battery-powered Geiger counter. I had absolutely no idea whether the feature was likely to be radioactive. There seemed no harm in checking it out. The local rock is granite so there would be some low-level background radiation, but the level of this could be checked away from the fairy highway.

My rods revealed that the barrier encircled the fairy thorn trees, enclosing an area around forty feet in diameter. From this circle emerged the fairy highway bounded by two barriers running parallel to each other about five feet apart. Nowhere along the entire length of the barriers was there any sign of abnormal radioactivity. At the fairy fort, the barrier enclosed a circular area this time over two hundred feet in diameter. As I proceeded, I stopped every so often to draw the line of the barrier as accurately as I could on the map.

Satisfied that I had mapped the full length of the feature and that there was little more that I could discover, I unpacked my lunch. I ate it on a smooth rock overlooking a fertile valley. It was very pleasant. As I ate, I mulled over what I knew. Looked at from first principles, my knowledge was very limited. All I really knew was that I could detect some sort of barrier with my divining rods and that it was not even a proper barrier because, without the rods, it just did not exist. Nor was it there if I carried both rods in the one hand. So, was it the rods or was it me that detected a barrier? Whatever the case, it was only supposition that it had anything to do with fairies. It could be anything. Perhaps it was some secret military project. Who knows what new technology might be involved? Perhaps it was Ireland's equivalent of Area 51. Maybe mysterious Mickey was just a delusional old man or just maybe he had been in contact with fairies. What was it he had spoken to Ciaran and written on the old newspaper? It took a few seconds for me to recall the words. *Clanwe yashpak!* Yes, *clanwe yashpak!* Without realising it, I said them aloud.

"Colhaboo." I heard a voice behind me and turned to see a man about five foot four tall who had a very pale complexion and wore a silver-coloured robe that appeared to be woven from some sort of metallic thread. "I beg your pardon," I said, "but who are you?"

"Call me Ixos," he replied. "Please tell me who you are, what are those metal rods, and how is it you speak my language?"

To tell the truth, at this point, I could not tell whether this was really happening or whether it was part of some weird dream. I told him to call me Tony and gave a detailed description of water divining. "But do you not detect other things with your rods?" he asked. This question disconcerted me and, rather than answer it, I asked why he had said that. "My companions and I have noticed disturbances to the perimeter of our domain that would seem to have been caused by your divining rods. We would like to investigate the matter."

Clearly, Ixos knew something of my encounters with the barrier, but just who was he? He did not appear to be in any way threatening. Indeed, his manner was very calm and relaxed. So, I described my experiences with the barrier both at Billy's plot and between the thorn tree and the fort. I explained that I had never previously encountered anything of that nature and enquired as to what exactly the barrier was and who exactly Ixos was.

Ixos stated that he would answer my questions but, before he did so, he would like me to answer his earlier question about my knowledge of his language. He listened intently to my explanation that *clanwe yashpak* were words I had come across recently. I said that I believed that they translated into "always strive for the greater good". I had no idea as to from what language they came and certainly did not know any other words from that language. Since Ixos pressed me for more information on just how I had come across the words, I outlined my conversation with Ciaran about Mickey.

The initial answers to my two questions left me just a little wiser. Ixos was a Carnacan. The barrier served to separate the domain in which Ixos lived from the rest of the world. It also protected from radiation emitted by the sun. The term Carnacan was meaningless to me. The bit about the barrier told me very little and did not seem very truthful. What use was a barrier if anyone could walk through it unless they happened to be carrying divining rods, which circumstance would so seldom occur as to be statistically insignificant? So, I embarked on a long series of questions. As the conversation continued, the realisation slowly dawned on me that Ixos would answer any question but would not volunteer information. Subsequently, I found that this was a character trait possessed also by his companions.

It transpired that a Carnacan was an inhabitant of Carnac, which is one of five planets orbiting a star which is part of the group we refer to as Cassiopeia. Carnac is of similar size to Earth and orbits its sun at a similar distance. Its surface has a greater proportion of land than Earth with land accounting for close to 60% of the total global area. The climate is broadly comparable to Earth's, although slightly cooler. This is due to differences in the radiation emitted by the two stars. The population has been stable for the past couple of thousand years at approximately 4.5 billion. Life expectancy is approximately 160 years. Carnacan years and Earth years differ little in duration.

Carnacan scientific knowledge and technology are much more advanced than its terrestrial equivalent. One consequence of this is that there is no requirement for most of the population to engage in any work. So, the practice has developed whereby the first twenty-five years of life are spent in study. Then, there followed twenty-five years of service to the greater good. The rest of Carnacan life is spent in what humans call retirement.

Ixos and his companions had come to Earth as part of a research project involving the study of humanity. I wanted to find out more about this project but, at this point, Ixos terminated the conversation. Understandably so, because we had been talking for several hours having spent a long time on the barrier.

I am still not sure that I can describe the science behind it correctly. I have always had an interest in scientific matters and have read widely on various topics, but I still find it difficult to comprehend some of the concepts involved. Carnacan scientists had long been aware of the apparent interchangeability of mass and energy. Like their human counterparts, they had observed wave-particle duality where the same entity appears to have the characteristics of a wave-like packet of energy and those of a solid particle. They found it puzzling that there should exist just two states that appear to be at the extreme ends of a wave-particle scale. Surely, some intermediate states should exist. Eventually, they discovered how to bring into being, for want of a better term, "stuff" that exists in an intermediate state. The properties of such stuff varied, depending on the proportions of the wave and particle in its composition. Initially, the inherent instability of the stuff proved problematic, rendering the stuff essentially useless. But, over time, various technological advances rendered the stuff more stable and enabled the prospective uses of the stuff to be exposed.

The stuff that the barrier consists of is around 8% particle and 92% wave energy and has remarkable properties. Firstly, it permits only some wavelengths of the electromagnetic spectrum to pass through, thereby acting as a filter. This solved one of the major problems regarding Carnacans spending time on Earth. They were aware that part of the solar radiation received on Earth was potentially very damaging to Carnacans. The barrier enabled Carnacans to spend unlimited time above ground on Earth without risk.

Whilst permitting passage of some radiation, the barrier is absolutely impenetrable to solid objects. At first, this seemed quite a nonsensical statement. Had I not walked through it without difficulty? Gradually, I obtained the full picture from Ixos. When I apparently walked through it, the barrier had altered shape as I moved forward. Essentially, it reduced its height from the normal eight feet down to less than a tenth of an inch thereby creating a path around three feet wide. I had actually walked over it. The first time I had entered inside the barrier was just before I heard Ixos speak to me. He had brought me inside the barrier, or rather he had shifted the barrier itself. I had been sitting on top of the barrier because it had flattened itself as I had entered the area around the fairy fort, which it covered. Ixos tried to explain the process whereby the barrier moved so that I was inside but, despite his repeated efforts, I still could not understand. The science was quite beyond me.

I also had great difficulty with the apparent invisibility of the barrier. According to Ixos, it is something akin to a one-way mirror. From inside the barrier, one can see what is outside the barrier without any hindrance but, from outside, one cannot see anything inside the barrier. Again, this seemed nonsensical until Ixos revealed that the barrier let light in but did not permit it to escape. The closest analogy is a greenhouse where the radiation, once it enters, is altered and partially retained. I suggested that there must be some other factor involved. If one cannot see through the barrier to what is inside, then the strip of ground under it should not be visible. And, yet it is. Ixos provided a very detailed explanation involving energy states and the differences between the outer and inner surfaces of the stuff. So, as far as I could understand, whereas the inner surface blocked the radiation by absorbing it, the outer surface deflected it. It was at this point that I finally realised the barrier had a floor as well as a ceiling. The radiation by which we see the ground underneath the barrier is bent around the barrier so that the ground is visible.

I was curious as to what happened to the grass growing in the area under the barrier. The explanation was that, whenever the field was being grazed by cattle or sheep, the barrier could be reshaped differently. Just as the barrier could be allowed to allow animals to cross, the two sides could be brought close together at times to allow all the grass to be grazed.

"What would happen," I asked, "if the farmer decides to bring in a machine to cut hay or silage?" Ixos thought that this would really stretch their ability to manipulate the barrier. As yet, it had not happened, but, if it ever did, he was confident they could cope.

It emerged that my interaction with the barrier had been a novel experience for the Carnacans. They were aware, from laboratory tests, that the stuff had differing reactions to various types of energy. The energy coming towards it was either allowed to pass through or blocked, depending on the electromagnetic frequency. However, energy passing over the surface of the barrier produced a range of reactions. Some types caused it to emit pulses of sound. Others increased the temperature of it. Yet others brought about a kind of fluorescence so that it became visible. My contact had occasioned not just an increase in temperature but also a temporary stiffening of the barrier. The Carnacans had not observed that previously.

When it first happened, the reaction had been picked up by their instruments, and two of the Carnacans had gone to the area of the barrier involved. They had observed my plotting the line of the barrier, my ascent of the col and my walk to the fairy thorn trees. They continued to watch me as I marked out the circle and then marked the course of the stream. They had been puzzled at my activity having never seen water divining before. When they first saw how the rods reacted to the barrier and later their different reaction as I walked the course of the stream, they then surmised that I must have been plotting some type of energy field.

Their curiosity had turned to apprehension whenever Billy had returned. As they listened to my suggestion that Billy resite his proposed house, the Carnacans could not understand initially why I was telling Billy a pack of lies. When they realised that I was trying to persuade him to site the house away from the barrier, they silently cheered me on. When Billy would not budge, their consternation was profound. A house built over the route to the thorn tree would render it unusable. Regular access to the tree was vital to them. If they were deprived of that access, it would cause them serious problems.

I had enquired whether the Carnacans could reroute the barrier away from the proposed site. Ixos said that while it could be done, it could not be achieved anytime soon. The difficulty was that they only had a small stock of the barrier material. Further supplies could be sent from Carnac, but it would not arrive in time.

When Ixos terminated the conversation, I was disappointed. He insisted it was for my own good that he was sending me home. I would understand in due course, he maintained. My only consolation was his agreement that I could return whenever I wished.

Having been told that the barrier would allow me to exit, I made my way home. My mind was in turmoil. Had I *really* just had a long conversation with an alien from outer space? Some of what he had told me was straight out of a science fiction novel. But the barrier was real, and Ixos had provided a coherent explanation no matter how fantastic some of it might be. Already, I was regretting not having asked about this or that topic, and I resolved to write a list of questions before my next visit. Included in them would be a few about Mickey. His mystery language was not that of the fairies but Carnacan. It was now obvious to me that Mickey had met Ixos or some of his companions, but that did not answer the questions concerning his age and his parents.

Several items of mail would meet me on my return home. This was unusual as one or two items per week were my normal quota. I set them aside to be read while I enjoyed a cup of coffee before preparing my evening meal. The coffee would have to be delayed as the carton of milk in the fridge was very obviously sour. It should not have been as I had bought it only the day previously, and there were still five days to go before its use-by date.

Not fancying black coffee, I headed to the nearby corner shop. Scrutiny of the dates on the milk revealed either 10 August or 12 August. But today was only 15 July. I had often wondered about use-by dates of up to seven or eight days removed, but this was becoming ridiculous. While taking the milk to the till, I happened to glance at the newspapers on sale. They were all dated 7 August! What on earth was going on? How had I lost 23 days?!

I took a copy and paid for it and the milk. Halfway back to the house, I realised that most of the contents of my fridge would be well past their use-by dates. I did not fancy a visit to the supermarket, so it was back to the corner shop to pay an inflated price for a bit of rib-eye steak, some tomatoes, celery, and baby potatoes.

On reaching home, switching on my computer revealed confirmation that today's date is 7 August.

My enjoyment of my coffee was ruined by the content of some of my letters. My credit card statement dated two days previously showed a hefty fee for non-payment of the previous bill.

It took some time for my state of shock to subside. As it did, some pieces of the jigsaw started to fall into place. If I had lost 23 days by spending a few hours within the barrier, then Mickey could well have lost time there as well. I had not shaved for 23 days, yet my face bore just the stubble that was normal for late evening. Ciaran had said that Mickey had been away for two and a half years. Going on what I had just experienced, that might only have been a couple of weeks within the barrier. If he had spent sufficient time within the barrier, it could well be that he had worked on the canal and had seen King William. I was truly excited and wanted to tell the whole world, but I realised I could not. People would think I was "away with the fairies." Just how apposite that comment would have been caused me to chuckle.

A short while later, I was forced into some off-the-cuff fib-telling. My landlord rang. When I heard his voice, I realised how fortunate I was that he was relaxed about collecting the rent. His usual practice was to ring and ask if I would be at home the following day. It could be four weeks between visits, or it could be as long as eighteen weeks. His last visit had been in late May. He had tried ringing me a couple of times during the previous week but got the message that my mobile was out of service. I told him it had been on the blink but now seemed OK and agreed to meet him the following day. I also took the opportunity to spin him a yarn about being offered some consulting work which would take me to either England or Malta for a couple of weeks at a time at irregular intervals. Perhaps the time had come for me to set up a standing order for the rent. Either that or I could make the payments via online banking. He agreed to bring details of a bank account with him the following day.

The next phone call was rather less cordial. "This is the last time I will lend you anything! Where have you been with my Geiger counter?" Tom was furious. Another friend was in the process of buying a house, one set in a beautiful location. He had heard that the owner of a bungalow nearby had experienced problems with a buildup of radon gas and had asked if Tom would check the house for radioactivity. Tom had advised him to contact the radon survey people. But as their checks would take between three and four weeks to produce results, he agreed to measure the background radiation in the house to set his friend's mind at rest. He was then unable to contact me to retrieve his Geiger counter. Furious was an inadequate description of his mood.

I felt guilty about lying to a friend of long-standing but could see no other way out of it. I invented a dash to the deathbed of an old uncle who had retired to Spain. He had lingered a couple of weeks longer than the doctors had anticipated. My phone had gone on the blink on the journey there. Tom was not mollified and demanded that I return the Geiger counter to his house the following morning.

The conversation left me feeling quite deflated. Even with careful planning situations like that were likely to occur if I was going to be absent for weeks at a time visiting the Carnacans. I would need to be extremely careful. Fortunately, I lived alone and was retired. Both my state pension and civil service pension were paid directly into my bank account. So, once I put in place arrangements to pay the rent online, enabling me to set up, weeks in advance, a payment for a particular date and set up a direct debit for my credit card account, I should be able to stay away for a few weeks at a time without too many problems.

Indeed, from a purely financial point of view, the situation was very beneficial. My income would be unaffected, but my expenditure would be dramatically reduced. During the past 23 days, my rent had accrued as normal, but I had spent nothing on food, nothing on drink, and my consumption of electricity had been minimal. Even looking at the cost of clothing, this should be greatly reduced if the clothes were going to last around sixty times longer than normal.

One complication was that I played bridge in three local clubs, two in Newry and one in Warrenpoint. The bridge season was due to resume in early September. So, I phoned each of my regular partners to inform them that I would be out of the country for a few weeks and was unsure as to when I would return. I promised to ring them as soon as I returned.

The next day was busy. After returning the Geiger counter, I paid the credit card bill and organised a direct debit for it. By good chance, it was blue and brown bin day, enabling me to get rid of food waste and dry recyclables. Whilst waiting for the landlord, I got busy with the Hoover and duster, finding it amazing just how dusty a house can become when it is neglected for over three weeks. Having put the house to rights, drawn up a list of questions for Ixos and eaten my evening meal, I took a notion to head to the Phoenix for a drink.

I arrived just in time to hear the latest scandal. One of the regulars was a security guard in the local government offices. He was able to tell us that the Chief Planning Officer was taking early retirement on health grounds. At least, that was the official version. One rumour had it that he had attempted suicide. Another version was that he was caught soliciting a bribe but was being treated leniently out of fear as to what might emerge if he were dismissed or prosecuted. I chose not to contribute to the discussion what I knew about his indebtedness to Billy, something about which the others present seemed completely unaware. It crossed my mind that the retirement lump sum would probably finish up in Billy's coffers because it was likely he would press the former Chief Planning Officer for payment now that he was no longer of any use to Billy.

As I sipped my glass of Rioja, I anticipated with pleasure the prospect of being able to tell Ixos that it was now most unlikely Billy would be able to build his house. I did not spend as long as I normally would in the pub as I did not enjoy having to deal with questions about where I had been during the past four weeks. It was not just that I had not been in the pub, but no one had seen me around town either. Rather than invent some foreign holiday, I just said it was great to have been missed.

Chapter 4

The following morning, having packed enough into the rucksack for three lunches, I headed for Knocknashee, rods under my arm. The same rock seemed as good a place as any to wait and see whether my arrival had been noticed. Sure enough, within a couple of minutes, Ixos appeared beside me.

"Welcome back," he said. After acknowledging his greeting, I indicated that before he described the research project on humanity, there were some other questions I wished to ask. "How did I lose 23 days between coming here and going home?" was my first question. "You did not," was the reply. The now-customary series of questions elicited the following explanation.

Having embarked on space exploration, the Carnacans sought to increase the distance they could travel. The limit of 25 years on serving the greater good meant that return trips could not be of any greater duration except for certain special projects. So, even if their spaceships could achieve speeds just shy of the speed of light and the voyagers spent very little time on the foreign planet, they were restricted to a radius of around twelve light years. Their spaceships could achieve almost 90% of light speed, but much of that speed was not usable. To avoid muscular atrophy on long trips, the ship had to rotate around the longitudinal axis to provide a measure of artificial gravityl. This rotation meant that the maximum speed of the ship was restricted to around 60% of light speed, which reduced the maximum radius of travel to around seven light years.

Their scientists knew that time did not always pass at a constant rate, appearing to pass more slowly at great velocities, but that effect was of limited benefit. They needed something with a much greater impact and, after decades of research and experimentation, found it in the shape of the time dilator. This is a device that causes time to pass more slowly within its sphere of influence. Ixos tried to explain how it works, but the explanation involved concepts well beyond my scientific understanding. The initial models brought the speed of time down to one-half of normal, but the devices kept burning out very quickly. The problem was that they tried to slow time down over infinite distances. Unless some method was discovered to limit their sphere of influence, they would not have any practical use. That remained the situation for several decades until the development of part particle, part energy stuff. This was found to be effective in enclosing the volume to be affected by the time dilator. Now that the device could be made to work effectively, the scientists sought to improve its performance. In the space of a few years, they achieved, first, one-quarter of the speed of time, then one-eighth, eventually reaching one-sixty-fourth of the speed of time. Their progress came to a halt as they found some sort of operator prevented any further time dilation.

The time dilator increased the radius of the sphere that could be explored during 25-yearlong trips to around 450 light years. The device was easily portable, meaning that it could be used on any planet they visited after a barrier containing the stuff had been constructed.

Once I had been brought inside the barrier, my life was running at one-sixty-fourth of the speed of time. Thus, during the eight and a half hours I experienced talking to Ixos, time outside the barrier had advanced by 23 days plus a few hours.

Back on Carnac, Ixos explained, part of the planet is on normal time speed while the rest runs at one-sixty-fourth time speed. In answer to my suggestion that surely everyone would want to live at a slower speed, he pointed out that there was no direct benefit to any person to be gained from living at a slower speed. The length of life any person experienced was exactly the same no matter at which time speed they lived. They did not gain any time. Their lives appeared to be longer to only those who live at a faster time speed.

Even before the time dilator had been properly developed, Carnacan scientists had foreseen its potential benefits in areas other than space travel. Think of a certain area of land sown with a grain crop. Once harvested, that grain would meet the needs of 1,000 people for a year. Now, suppose those 1,000 people are living at one-sixty-fourth of the speed of time. That same quantity of grain will meet not just their needs but also the needs of another 63,000 people living at that slower time speed. This method of feeding additional people works only if the grain is grown at a faster time speed than that in which the consumers live.

Similar considerations can be applied to animals reared for consumption. A herd which would provide meat for 10,000 people would instead feed 640,000. Fish stocks would also benefit. The greatly reduced consumption eliminates the problem of overfishing keeping the fish population at a healthy level.

All of this is achieved without any detrimental effect on the diet of the population.

Of course, it is impossible to have the entire population living at a slower time speed. Someone has to grow the crops, raise the animals and go to sea in the fishing boats. But the great majority can live at a slower time speed. Currently, on Carnac, just 15% of the population lives at normal speed. This means that the area of land under tillage is just one-sixth of what it would otherwise be. Similarly, the number of farmed animals is also only one-sixth of what would otherwise be needed, also reducing the land needed for grazing.

A further benefit is a healthier environment. Greenhouse gases are reduced by five-sixths. This is of major importance insofar as methane from farm animals is involved as it is one of the more potent greenhouse gases. Nor is the reduction in carbon dioxide insignificant. Not only is the amount produced by Carnacan respiration and industrial activity reduced by five-sixths, but the smaller area needed for farming enables the use of additional forest and woodland to help remove carbon dioxide from the atmosphere.

"So!" Ixos proclaimed. "The time dilator is, without a doubt, the greatest-ever invention."

I did not disagree, but I was wondering how the Carnacans managed to move the food from one time speed to the other.

From my, admittedly, limited understanding of the method by which Ixos brought me inside the barrier, I could not see that the same method would be practical for truckloads of food. For once, my thinking was correct but overlooked a very obvious solution to the problem. On Carnac, there is no requirement to keep the existence of the stuff barriers secret since all knew about them. Thus, they were able to construct the time speed equivalent of airlocks at any boundary between the two zones. These were equipped with time dilators that were kept switched off when supplies entered from the normal time speed and switched on when the supplies were transferred to the other zone.

All of this made sense, but one question still bugged me. I had sat within the barrier for over 23 days, and during that time, the view of the countryside outside had not altered. Why had I not witnessed dusk, night, dawn and daylight for each of those days? "A mild deception," said Ixos. "We did not wish you to be aware of the time dilator at that stage. What you saw throughout that visit was an artificial projection."

I now had some understanding of what had happened at my last visit and was happening again this time. The science behind the dilator was utterly beyond my comprehension and Ixos had abandoned his attempts to explain it, but I felt a lot happier. It was also good to finally know the truth about Mickey as Ixos answered my questions on the subject.

This is what happened, according to Ixos: "Mickey had visited the Carnacans on many occasions and stayed with them for varying lengths of time. His entry into their domain had come in more dramatic circumstances than mine. As Ixos explained, no technology, however advanced, is ever perfect. There is always the possibility, however remote, of some kind of malfunction. Such a malfunction occurred just eight Earth years after they arrived to replace the previous group. Part of the barrier went down. Most of the time, this would not be a major problem. The main parts surrounding Knocknashee, and the fairy thorn trees were still functional, and the fault would be quickly rectified. But Citas, one individual in the group, had just embarked on a walk down to the fairy thorn trees, and the field through which he was passing contained a bull. At the sudden appearance of this person in his territory, the bull charged. Citas was caught unawares and went down under the impact. He was not gored but sustained internal injuries. Fortunately, Mickey happened to be close by and came running over as the bull tried to attack Citas again but now as he was lying on the ground. Mickey drove off the bull using his blackthorn stick.

Ixos continued: "Citas was dressed in a Carnacan metallic robe, so Mickey knew he was not an ordinary human. He lifted Citas in his arms and carried him towards where Ixos and I sat, asking the groaning Citas: 'How do we get you back into the fairy fort?' We knew that Citas needed urgent attention, so we opened the entrance to our underground living quarters. Mickey was unfazed. He kept repeating, 'I knew the fairies were real.'" Ixos kept going: "We did not disillusion Mickey. Had he asked us directly if we were fairies, we would have told him we were not, but he never did. We knew very little about fairies apart from that they were some kind of otherworldly beings who possessed magical powers. We felt a debt of gratitude to Mickey. Without his actions, Citas could have been more severely injured or even killed. So, we allowed him to visit whenever he wished. This he did frequently but, unlike you, he did not ask many questions. Anything he saw which was beyond his comprehension or normal experience, he attributed to fairy magic. We went along with it as it suited our purposes. We did not wish humanity to be aware of our presence or the reasons for it, although we always knew that it might be unavoidable for some human to discover us."

Listening to Ixos describe, in that deadpan manner of his, Mickey's belief that the Carnacans were fairies, I was only too aware that it could easily be me he was describing. On my initial encounter with the barrier, my thinking had been that the explanation involved fairies.

"So, when did the incident with the bull occur?" I asked. Ixos said he could check their records but that, as he remembered, it was around nine Earth years following their arrival in 1660. It had been a horrible time in Europe and the British Isles. It had been so bad that they considered assisting humanity with Carnacan medicine. They did not intervene due to a realisation that it would be a futile exercise. Storage constraints on spaceships meant that they had brought limited medical supplies. Certainly, the quantity available would be sufficient for only a few thousand out of the millions who were infected.

Ixos's account meant that it was around 1668 or 1669 when Mickey had saved Citas. Further questioning established that Mickey had claimed to be thirty years of age at the time, which put his birth before the great plague. He had been around 370 when he died. Small wonder none of his neighbours could remember his parents. Ciaran would be utterly amazed to hear that the account of King William passing with his army was actually a first-hand one. It was a shame that I felt unable to tell him.

That started me wondering why the Carnacans were allowing me access to them. Were they not running a major risk that I would reveal their presence to the rest of the world? If I brought witnesses to Billy's land, I could demonstrate the presence of the barrier especially if I was able to arrange for Johnny to be there so that he and I could each get the same reaction from either side of the barrier. The Carnacans would not be aware of what was happening until too late.

"But you would not do that," said Ixos. His statement startled and disconcerted me. Had I unwittingly spoken my thoughts aloud? It transpired that thought-reading was the reason for such confidence on the part of Ixos. A person can lie in conversation, but he can never lie in his thoughts. I started to express my wonderment at his ability but was informed it was nothing special. It was not just Carnacans who could read thoughts, but various animals could do it to a limited extent. Dogs were one species he cited as an example.

The techniques involved were extremely basic but, as with many skills, required considerable practice before they could be mastered. Before I left Knocknashee, I was starting to get the hang of the thought-reading techniques.

At this point, Ixos suggested that we should have something to eat. He confirmed that our digestive systems and general biochemistry were sufficiently similar to enable either of us to eat each other's food. He was curious about the food I had brought. He would not be the first to wonder about my choices. Some of my friends used to laugh frequently about my idiosyncratic tastes. On this occasion, the three types of sandwiches in my rucksack were corned beef and tomato made with paninis, cucumber, red pepper, and celery made in soda farls and a more conventional ham and cheese in wheat bread. These would be washed down with either orange juice or red wine and followed by a banana and a pear or nectarine.

Perhaps his tastes were as unusual as mine because Ixos accepted my invitation for him to share my picnic. Whilst we ate, there occurred a sort of role reversal as Ixos quizzed me about my life. He appeared quite conversant with many aspects of human life, which I did not find particularly surprising if he was engaged in a study of humanity. The one thing that seemed to puzzle him was my attempt at humour when I outlined my previous employment. My first employment had been as a laboratory technician with the Blood Transfusion Service, and I later became an Inspector of Taxes, so I said I had gone from one vampire squad to another. Even when I explained the reference to Bram Stoker's novel, his deadpan expression did not alter. However, he did show great interest in the subject of taxation, saying that he would like to question me further about it on some later occasion.

Nor did he display any emotion when I remembered to deliver the good news about Billy's building project. I had expected him to be delighted and perhaps he was, although he did not show it. "That is good. Thank you for the information," was his deadpan response.

When we had finished eating, I started questioning him regarding the research project involving the study of humanity.

Before we began this part of our conversation, I had not given much thought to the age of Carnacan civilisation. Their technology was clearly significantly more advanced than ours, so their civilisation was likely to be more ancient. But all I had was a pretty vague notion that it predated ours by a few thousand years. So, the discovery that Carnac had a stable, well-developed civilisation 45,000 years ago came as a shock. We tend to pride ourselves on the great advances humanity has made, particularly during the past two hundred years. But our history and achievements pale into insignificance when compared to those on Carnac.

Forty-three thousand years ago, Carnacan scientific knowledge and technology were already, in many areas, more advanced than human knowledge and technology in the early twenty-first century. Their agricultural practices were also well in advance as was their medical knowledge. But even with all that, they were unable to avert the disaster which befell them.

A virus struck. One the like of which was never encountered either previously or since. To describe it in human terms, it was much more contagious than either the black death or the Spanish flu, and its mortality rate exceeded that of Ebola. Even the most stringent precautions seemed to offer little defence. Medical scientists were unable to develop effective vaccines. Pre-existing anti-viral treatments were ineffective, and they could not develop new treatments quickly enough. In just a couple of years, the planet's population was devastated. Before the virus, the population was around 5 billion. In the aftermath, it stood at just over 155,000.

The next few years were all about survival, and this was far from guaranteed. Those who had survived were scattered all over the planet. Some of the groups of survivors were probably too small to be viable in the long term. The main communication networks were no longer functioning, rendering organised action difficult. Worst of all, even after the pandemic had subsided, serious health hazards remained. Many corpses lay decaying in homes and former hospitals. Even though they had not been directly affected by the virus, many farm animals had died from starvation, and their carcases littered the land.

Gradually, the survivors managed to contact each other and formulate a recovery plan. They all moved to one area of around 1,000 square miles. It was a very fertile area that had been primarily devoted to tillage and had been relatively sparsely populated. This meant that there were fewer corpses to be disposed of than in other areas. The normal practice had been burial but, of necessity, they now used mass cremations. Collecting the bodies and burning them was a gruesome task, but it needed to be done.

Once the corpses had been cleared from their chosen area, they focussed on bringing agriculture back into shape and expanding the two pre-existing towns to provide sufficient and good-quality accommodations. Bit by bit, as progress was made, they restarted various industries. It was a slow process.

When formulating the recovery plan, the survivors were very conscious that they had a very small gene pool. They knew that it was not just interbreeding between close relatives that could cause problems. There had been instances in the past where even comparatively large island communities had suffered from the effects of a limited gene pool. They were fortunate that one of their numbers was a geneticist. He assembled a small team and took samples from every person, except females who were too old to breed. The team braved the horrendous trip to the nearest city containing a laboratory with the equipment required to obtain a DNA profile for each person. The next step was to plan a breeding programme designed to maintain the greatest genetic diversity possible with such a small population. And, thus, they started the genetic register of all Carnacans. The register is maintained to this very day.

As the population increased, it became possible to repopulate the planet one area at a time. As the years passed, the task of clearing the corpses from an area became a lot easier because all that remained were skeletons. However, the population growth was much slower than the survivors had anticipated. They had started with around 30,000 females of reproductive age and another 14,000 who were below reproductive age. When almost a third of these failed to conceive, investigations revealed that those who had been infected by the virus and recovered had been left infertile. Only those who had avoided the virus altogether could breed. Fortunately, the same problem did not affect the males. Even so, thousands of years passed before the population recovered to around 80% of its pre-virus level. At that point, the decision was made to maintain the population at that level.

In pre-virus days, Carnacans were in the early stages of exploring their solar system. They had set up a base on the next planet out. Its principal purpose was to conduct astronomical observations using different parts of the electromagnetic spectrum. Making the observations 35 million miles from Carnac obviated the problems with light pollution and other electromagnetic radiation emanating from cities and industries on the home planet. A crew of five were serving a tour of duty there when the virus hit. They were intended to return to Carnac around three months later. Two days before they were due to start the journey back, the space centre instructed them to stay where they were. With twelve months' worth of food at the base, this did not present a major difficulty. Each day, the crew listened to the account from the space centre of the worsening situation on Carnac. Four months after the instruction to stay at the base, the space centre ceased communications. The crew suspected there was no one left alive at the centre.

They decided to ration the remaining food to prolong their stay for a further fifteen months. This was partly in the hopes that the space centre would become operative again. If it did not, they wanted to wait as long as possible before returning to Carnac to increase the chance that the virus had been brought under control. Little did they suspect that, by the time they returned, the pandemic would be just about over but only because the virus had effectively run out of potential victims.

Their journey back to Carnac was the stuff of legend. Never before had a crew come back from outer space without the benefit of a constant flow of data and guidance from the space centre.

Even to guide their craft back to the vicinity of Carnac was a major achievement. It required a combination of great skill and good fortune to re-enter the atmosphere at precisely the correct angle, and they landed safely. The five were among those principally responsible for the success of the recovery plan.

Understandably, that was the last space flight for many, many years. The space exploration programme was abandoned and only resumed around 30,000 years later. Upon its resumption, it was restricted, at first, to their solar system. Later, developments in propulsion technology allowed them to travel further afield. Then, some 3,000 years ago, the development of the time dilator and particle-energy stuff enabled more space exploration to begin in earnest.

As the programme progressed, the Carnacans observed the various life forms that had evolved on different planets. Most were primitive but, on a small number of planets, Carnacan-like species were present. These were the only species to have acquired much in the way of technology albeit mostly very basic when compared to that on Carnac. One of these species was humanity. Human technology was at this point pretty primitive, but it was heading in the right direction.

The Carnacans had continuing concerns about the limited diversity in their genetic pool and, for this reason, had maintained the planned breeding programme. They reasoned that if any of these species proved suitable, it would provide a welcome increase in genetic diversity. Some information could be obtained by remote observation but whether the biochemistry of the species was sufficiently compatible required direct physical examination, including scans, chemical analyses, and dissection. To this end, ten of each species were captured and transported back to Carnac. Each was scanned, and their blood and other bodily fluids were analysed. Finally, they were anaesthetized, and their lives were extinguished before dissection. A total of twenty-three species were examined. With most, the resemblance to Carnacans proved to be superficial. With some, the internal structures were quite different, and, with others, the biochemistry was totally incompatible. Only three were sufficiently similar to permit interbreeding with Carnacans. One of these species was humanity.

The physical examination was just the first phase of the process. An equally important part was the psychological evaluation of the species. Carnac had a very orderly society, and the Carnacans wished it to remain so. The conduct of any such evaluation presented many difficulties. Unlike the physical examination, it could not be undertaken on Carnac. Removing a person from their natural environment and transporting them to another planet would cause immense psychological stress and render any conclusions invalid. Nor could the process be carried out quickly. It required the observers to understand how the species communicated. This entailed learning to comprehend their language without the benefit of any teacher. For the evaluation to be valid, the species had to be unaware that it was taking place. As such, the language had to be deciphered without any native assistance. It was also understood that actions could be misinterpreted unless those actions could be examined in the proper context. To enable these, a study of the species' environment, behaviour, and interaction with each other was required.

Carnacans were understandably very cautious. The eventual decision to interbreed with another species could have unforeseen consequences. As such, the correct decision needed to be made. Accordingly, the observations and data collected were required to be as comprehensive as possible. The species would need to be observed through many generations.

The plan required setting up four hundred observation posts on each of the three planets. Each post would have a complement of ten males or females. As a Carnacan spaceship could accommodate forty people, one ship would be required for each four bases. The tour of duty would allow the observers to spend twelve years on Earth. Because this tour would be spent at one-sixty-fourth of the speed of time, it would cover 768 years or around twenty-five human generations. The first batch of two hundred bases on Earth was instituted around 2,700 years ago. This base was part of the second batch created four hundred years later.

Each base is of similar design with minor variations occasioned by the local terrain. This seemed strange as I could not see the sense in having an outpost like the one at the fairy thorn trees with a long connecting highway. The explanation concerned communication and yet another piece of Carnacan technology. Even before the development of the time dilator, Carnacan spaceships were travelling up to several light years away from home. Because electromagnetic radiation can travel no faster than the speed of light, communication between the space centre and spaceship was so slow as to be virtually useless. It required decades of research before the sub-ethereal transmitter was invented. This enabled a message to travel from transmitter to receiver, over any distance and almost instantaneously. It was not a complete solution to the problem. One insurmountable difficulty was that sub-ethereal transmission caused a backwash of energy which, whilst harmless to people, caused serious damage to hypertronic equipment. The damage could occur up to 1,000 feet away from the transmitter. A land-based transmitter could easily be sited well away from any susceptible equipment, but that was not possible on a spaceship. A vessel of the size required for such a separation could not be built. Still, the reception of sub-ethereal messages did not suffer from the same problem so messages from the space centre could be transmitted instantaneously, thereby halving the time required for communications. Sub-ethereal communication then came into its own with the establishment of observation bases. The transmitter for the base at Knocknashee is sited at the fairy thorn trees. Hence, it is an absolute necessity that the route inside the barrier is always available to the Carnacans.

The scale and duration of this observation exercise left me almost speechless. Looking back, I still find it strange that I felt no resentment at my species being treated like goldfish in a bowl or animals in one of the earlier zoos. Perhaps the thought that Carnacan scientists were investigating whether humanity could improve their genetic pool engendered a sense of pride rather than annoyance. Instead, I wondered how Carnac could land a fleet of fifty large spaceships at sites spread right around the world without being detected. It was not as if the observation sites were in remote inaccessible regions. They were all in inhabited regions to enable the study of the local populations. What about earlier fleets, the one that arrived in 1980 must surely have been noticed. Didn't the US and USSR have space exploration capabilities at the time?

I was partially correct in my thinking. In most circumstances, the spaceships are effectively invisible. Due to the need to contain the sphere of influence of the time dilator, the ship has an outer skin of the stuff from which the barrier is constructed; so, light, radar, etc. simply bend around it. The only time the ship becomes in any way visible is during entry to a planet's atmosphere. Human spacecraft re-enter Earth's atmosphere behind thick heat shields, which are burnt away by the tremendous heat generated by the friction encountered upon re-entry. Carnacan vessels do not use heat shields. The vessels have been designed to manage the extreme temperatures without them. The heat energy just flows along the ship's "skin." Now the amount of heat energy generated is dependent on the angle of entry into the atmosphere. Change that angle by a fraction of a degree and the heat energy can dramatically increase. That increase can be sufficient to bring the heat energy flow along the ship's barrier skin above the threshold at which the stuff fluoresces and becomes visible.

On average, around one in ten Carnacan spacecraft exhibits this fluorescence on entry into Earth's atmosphere. It is a short-lived phenomenon persisting for anywhere from a few seconds to a minute, mostly the shorter time. It has been witnessed by humans down through the centuries and has been variously attributed to chariots of the gods or shooting stars. The sightings in 1980 contributed to the widespread interest in UFOs. Governments and military commanders around the world were mystified. Whatever these things were, they had been briefly visible to the naked eye but did not show on any radar screen. At the time, both the US and USSR were seeking to develop stealth-fighter-plane technology, and the mutual suspicion was intense.

"Did all the spacecraft arrive safely on Earth?" I asked. "And did they all reach Carnac safely on their return journey?" The answer was no. Two spaceships had been lost on entering Earth's atmosphere, both in similar circumstances. One had been part of the fifth fleet to arrive, and the other was one of the fleet with which Ixos and his companions had arrived in 1660. The Carnacans are not certain of the cause of each incident. Most likely, pilot error was involved, but some glitch with the navigational system cannot be entirely discounted. In the 1660 incident, the angle of entry was so far out that the heat energy became so intense that the deflective flow along the surface of the vessel was insufficient to prevent a rapid build-up of heat within the vessel. The heat caused a component of the propulsion control system to fail, leaving the spaceship at the mercy of its residual velocity and the effects of Earth's gravity. All the other ships had received the sub-ethereal transmission to the space centre that would not have been sent unless the captain knew the vessel was doomed. Calculations based on its entry speed, angle of flight and Earth's gravity suggested it had crashed into a deep lake in eastern Africa. And, as much as the Carnacans would have wished to recover the remains of those on board, such a recovery mission was not feasible. To begin with, the equipment necessary would need to be transported from Carnac and some of that equipment would have to be partially disassembled to fit inside a spaceship. Reassembling it would be a difficult task, requiring the transport of engineers from Carnac. There was no guarantee that the recovery would succeed, but what was guaranteed was that the operation could not be carried out without being witnessed by humans.

The other spaceship lost had crashed in the middle of the ocean. The location of both crash sites mitigated against human discovery. And, even if, by some remote chance, some submarine passed close by, the spaceship would be invisible to human eyes as the outer skin of barrier material would still be intact; it can withstand any impact.

"Where is the spaceship on which you travelled?" I asked. "Antarctica" was the monosyllabic reply. Further probing revealed that the spaceships did not return to Carnac during the crew's stay at the observation base. There were two reasons for this.

One was the duration of the trip back to the home planet. The pilot would be alone on the ship. The only communication he would enjoy would be receiving one-way messages from the space centre or chatting via radio with the other pilots in the fleet on the same journey. Several years in such a situation was an unattractive prospect.

More importantly, it would have left those stationed on the bases with no method to leave Earth should anything untoward occur. A rescue ship despatched from Carnac would take years to arrive, and that would most likely be too late.

It was not possible to park the spaceship beside any of the four bases occupied by those it had brought. Yes, it would be effectively invisible, but its perimeter could not be left flexible like the barriers at the bases. Beneath the barrier skin was a rigid structure. Nor could it be brought within the barrier as the same consideration applied. So, the initial practice was for all the pilots, after disembarking their passengers and cargo, to rendezvous at remote locations far away from human habitation. There they set up a base for them, with groups of twenty sharing the accommodation in one of the ships. During their stay, their observation work primarily concerned geology and climate.

The first few fleets set up base in the Siberian wilderness but latterly they favoured the least-populated continent of Antarctica.

Having learnt about the history and reason behind the observation project, I was keen to discover what the Carnacans thought about humanity. This was the first question that Ixos refused to answer. Actually, he did not quite but said he would need to discuss with Carnac how much, if anything, he could reveal to me about their findings. He could provide no firm answer as to how long his consultation with Carnac might take.

It might be completed quickly, or it could take days, and he was referring to slow-time-speed days.

I was disappointed but there was nothing I could do about it. I did try the cheeky approach and asked if I could see inside the base. Ixos replied that he had been hoping I would ask because they would like to run some tests on the energy involved in my use of the divining rods.

Whatever Ixos did to open the entrance to the base, I did not spot it. Part of the surface of the ground seemed to fold downwards and to one side revealing a flight of shallow steps leading underground. He made no move to enter the opening but instead spoke to a companion inside. Their conversation in Carnacan was incomprehensible to me. The second Carnacan emerged from underground carrying a black cuboid item, which was around two feet high, one foot wide and six inches deep. On what I assumed was its front, there were various circular and square clear panels. Behind some of these were flashing illuminated shapes whilst others possessed what looked like clock faces. My guess was this was some sort of measuring device.

Ixos introduced me to Citas, who asked if I could stand at a certain spot with a divining rod in each hand. He then attached electrodes to the rods, my hands, arms, torso, and ankles. On being told to step forward, my rods swung up vertically, and I realised I was touching the inside of the barrier. This was repeated several times with Citas moving the electrodes or employing different electrodes. In due course, he expressed his satisfaction and the three of us moved underground.

We had only descended three steps when Citas spoke to Ixos in Carnacan. Ixos stopped and said we were going to return to the surface to check something. Once back on the surface, Citas asked me if he could try using my divining rods. I willingly agreed, but Citas obtained no reaction whatsoever from touching the barrier. Neither did Ixos. The temptation to say "At least there is one thing I can do better than Carnacans" was irresistible. Neither of them laughed or even smiled, but they did not seem to be offended either. Both just nodded and murmured in agreement.

We then descended a total of thirty steps, which were in two flights with a landing and a 180-degree turn halfway. At the bottom was a rectangular area around twenty feet by fifteen feet with various doors leading off it. We entered through the sole door on the short side facing us into a large room about thirty feet by thirty feet. From a height of around three feet, up to the ceiling, which I estimated to be just over eight feet high, the walls were lined with what looked like television screens. There were two arrays of television screens, standing as high as the ceiling, that were supporting both sides of a twelve-foot-by-twelve-foot stand in the centre of the room. Each screen was fifteen inches^2 so, by my reckoning, there were about six hundred screens. The image on each screen was different and appeared to change once every five seconds.

Glancing at the different images on each screen, I recognised one scene. It was Hill Street in Newry. Not far away was a screen showing English Street in Armagh, and I also recognised West Street in Drogheda. Unlike typical CCTV footage, the images were remarkably clear. I discovered that the base had devices recording both visual images and sound spread all over the northern half of the island. The images were recorded at fifty frames per second. Having been filmed at normal time speed, displaying them live in a slow-time-speed area would have been like trying to watch something fast forward. Hence, the single image every five seconds.

It would be impractical to watch everything that was recorded, but there was no need to do so. By now, the Carnacans had an enormous archive showing routine life in all parts of the world. The system was now programmed to flag instances of certain types of behaviour. It would also flag certain sounds or spoken words. Although not everything was viewed, all recordings were stored in case they needed to be viewed as part of the study. Citas produced a storage device that was about an inch and a half by three-quarters of an inch and very thin, somewhere around one-fortieth of an inch. Each storage device held around 20,000 hours. The recordings were duplicated. One set was kept at the base while the duplicate would be brought taken to Carnac when the crew returned there after their tour of duty.

For most of the recording sites, the archive dated back to within a few years of the establishment of the base 5,480 years ago. For some sites, the recordings' commencement was more recent, as many urban centres only came into being much later. A small settlement mushroomed, in the twelfth century, into a town, later the city, of Newry. Similarly, other towns, such as Portadown and Lurgan, only came into existence in the early eighteenth century. By contrast, the recording at some of the original sites had become redundant. Newgrange near Drogheda and the Navan Fort outside Armagh were two such examples.

This was a truly remarkable archive of human existence on the island of Ireland, which was replicated all over the globe. One of the things that amazed me was that the entire record for the island of Ireland, from the earliest recording onwards, would fit in a shoebox.

Whilst we were talking about the recording sites, I quipped that it was good to know that I had appeared on Carnacan television and not just on one channel. Most recent recordings of me would be from Newry, but there would be a lot of older recordings from Armagh where I spent my youth, with Belfast, Newcastle and Dunleer featuring heavily during intervening years. There might even be recordings from London and Manchester where I had lived before moving to Armagh at three years of age. Recording in London was the least likely because my family had moved to Manchester shortly after my first birthday. Later London recordings might be available regarding various trips I had made to that city from the age of thirty onwards. Citas replied that they were already aware of all of this.

He activated one of the blank screens on the central island, and there appeared footage of English Street in Armagh. At first, the street was deserted, which suggested late evening, night time, or possibly it was a Sunday. Then two people emerged from the door of the Vintage Bar, walking hand in hand. "Lover-boy Tony" observed Ixos. I was with Theresa, my girlfriend back in 1975. I blushed as we watched Theresa and I stop for a passionate kiss, her arms around my neck, one arm of mine drawing her close while the other hand moved over her posterior.

Citas stopped the recording and brought up another one and announced, "Now, soldier Tony." I laughed. Certainly, I was dressed in a grey military uniform, but it was that of the Order of Malta Ambulance Corps of which I had been a member. I was holding a collection tin during an annual street collection, or Flag Day, as it would then have been called. Citas and Ixos quizzed me about the Order of Malta. They had not been aware of its existence, assuming that people in uniform belonged to the military.

As he brought up the next recording, Citas said, "People have called you Anthony." Before I could reply, I was watching another recording on English Street. The recording was even older than the previous two as one could see a toy shop named The Jolly Roger, which ceased trading during my teens. It was my mother and me. As we appeared, Citas activated the sound, and we heard my mother's voice, with its residual trace of a Salford accent, say "Those last potatoes from the vegetable man weren't great. Quinn's has the new Cyprus ones in. You go in and get half a stone while I go to the butcher." "Yes, Mammy," I replied as she handed me a half-crown before I headed to Quinn's The Milestone whilst she went into Flanagan's butcher shop. A couple of minutes later, I reappeared carrying the potatoes and stood waiting outside the butcher shop until my mother emerged.

It would not be an exaggeration to describe me as utterly flabbergasted. How on Earth, or even on Carnac, had they been able to link that old footage to me? The explanation began with facial recognition technology. This enabled the system to be programmed so all recordings of the same person could be identified. Next, enhancement of the technology enabled predictive ageing of a subject. They could programme the system to show how the person would look at various times in the future. The technology was not perfect as certain factors, such as surgery, facial scarring or excessive weight gain, could cause it to fail, but it had a phenomenally high success rate. Further experimentation enabled reverse ageing to be applied. They had images of me from my initial visit to Bill's site so there had been ample time for them to review the many images recorded at various sites and select some to show me.

The system also flagged images recorded by other bases. "What did you think of the ruins of Troy?" asked Citas, as we watched a recording of me visiting the ruins whilst on holiday in Turkey. Next, we saw me crossing the reconstructed bridge in Mostar.

There were other features at which to marvel about their technology. The audio could be tweaked to isolate speech by one or more persons whilst silencing background noise. This they had done with the clip of my mother and me. A translation into Carnacan could be dubbed on the recording without affecting the original soundtrack, and any user could choose which to use. This meant that only a small number of Carnacans needed to learn any particular terrestrial language.

I was curious about whether any recording device had been discovered by a human and whether any had ceased to function or been damaged by human or animal activity. Citas explained that the devices were very small, and the exterior could be customised to blend in with the background. None of the devices used by this base had ever been discovered, but there had been instances in other parts of the world. Whenever that happened, the device could be switched off remotely. So far, there was no indication that any of the finders had figured out what the device was. Around one per cent of the devices malfunctioned over time, which represented quite a low failure rate. This left the great majority of even the oldest devices still operative. Ever since the beginning of the project, devices had been damaged by animal activity. It had never happened in Ireland but in other parts of the world, some animals, such as chimpanzees, had been known to run off with the devices. By contrast, damaged caused by human activity was almost unknown until recent times. The first occasion a device used by this base was so damaged was in 1690 in Londonderry. The impact of a cannonball on a building dislodged the device and, from the images it continued to send, it appeared to be lying on the ground. After a few minutes, it ceased to operate, and Citas reckoned it had been trodden underfoot or run over by a cart's wheel. The next instance was in Dublin in 1916 when another was damaged in the fighting that took place. Another was lost when the German Luftwaffe bombed Belfast in 1941. Four more were destroyed during the 1970s. Two were in Belfast, one in Dungannon and the other in Monaghan with an explosion being the cause on each occasion.

"So, what did you do?" I asked. "Did you replace the devices, and how were you able to do so? Indeed, how did you install the devices in the first place?" All the devices used by this base had been replaced, although Citas explained that replacing them was not essential. The Carnacans aimed to record sufficient human activity to allow them to successfully complete their study of humanity. To achieve that aim, they needed a certain number of recording devices, but, since they had installed well more than that number, the loss of a few was of no major importance.

The original installation of the devices and the subsequent replacement of a few of them required Carnacans to exit the protective shield of the barrier. In the absence of other measures, they would become exposed to harmful solar radiation during any daylight hours they spent outside. Additionally, they would be outside the slow-time-speed zone. A third problem was the risk of being seen by humans. These problems had been foreseen when the project was being planned, and the Carnacans had designed a vehicle capable of transporting two people and a small amount of equipment. It could travel either on four wheels or in hover mode to suit the terrain it was traversing. In either mode, it could achieve speeds of up to 100 mph. Crucially, it was covered by a skin of the barrier, rendering it both invisible and capable of carrying a time dilator. Using the vehicle, the installation or replacement of a device now required a Carnacan to be at normal time speed for only a few seconds that the operation took. If these few seconds passed during the hours of darkness, the risk of harm from solar radiation was eliminated. A slight risk of being seen remained; Citas had been seen on one occasion. He was just about to re-enter the vehicle after he had replaced a device in Monaghan, and then a human staggered round the corner. Citas entered the vehicle as quickly as he could, and he and his companion watched and listened as the man stood swaying, open-mouthed, looking in the direction where he had seen Citas suddenly disappear. They reckoned that, since he was intoxicated, the man was going to be in no way sure that he had seen what he thought he had seen and might not recall the incident. The words he had been recorded as saying made little sense to them, and Ixos asked if I would listen to them. Citas located and played the recording. I laughed as I listened the drunk say to himself, "I am definitely taking the pledge!" The existence of the Pioneers was a new piece of information for Ixos and Citas.

The vehicle served another purpose. The Carnacans wished to record events that appeared to be of major importance to humans. They reckoned that any event in which a large number participated or that was watched by a large number was significant. Such events were infrequent until the late nineteenth century when the number started to increase. Having recorded numerous events that involved either thirty-one or twenty- three men and a sphere or ovoid, the Carnacans still could not understand the significance of the events. Nor had they yet worked out why around one million people had assembled in Phoenix Park Dublin in 1932. Events of a similar nature had occurred around the world from the late 1970s onwards.

I tried to explain football but, the more I tried, the less comprehending Ixos and Citas appeared. Eventually I reached the conclusion that they just did not understand the concept of competitive sport. With that realisation, I thought there was little point in trying to explain religious gatherings.

The usefulness of the vehicle was very restricted in that it could be used to record only outdoor events. It would be too risky for it to enter any building, and no Carnacan had ever been inside any human building. As a consequence, Carnacans thought that there were whole areas of human activity regarding which they had little information. This belief was confirmed when humans began broadcasting electromagnetic waves. At first, the waves could be converted only into sound by a receiver, but soon they carried visible images as well. Much of the sound-only broadcasts consisted of sound sequences that followed some type of mathematical pattern with varying degrees of repetition, and some of the sound recordings accompanying visual images were of similar nature. Their study of the sound sequences accompanying the visual images revealed that the sounds were produced in a variety of ways. Some were produced by the passage of air through wooden or metal tubes of various shapes, others by striking objects of either metal or animal skin. Yet, others were made by the human voice – either a single voice or a number of voices – and frequently, there was a combination of all methods. "What are these sound sequences, and why are they so important to humans?" Ixos asked.

Explaining playing music and singing was not going to be easy especially as my rather tuneless singing voice would render any attempt at demonstration pointless. Just as I was about to begin my attempt, the thought struck me: Why should I? They won't tell me what they think about humanity. Why should I fill in any more gaps in their knowledge? It should be a two-way street. It was difficult to assess their reaction to my statement that I would need time to consider whether I should explain sound sequences. They seemed neither annoyed nor surprised but merely requested my reason. When this was conveyed to them, Ixos suggested that I go home and return at my convenience when we could assess how things stood.

On my way home, nagging doubts surfaced in my mind. What if the Carnacans refused to allow me any more contact? These doubts did not disappear altogether but were greatly reduced by the realisation that the Carnacans needed me, or some other human, if they were to have any hope of really understanding humanity. The fact that they had no understanding of music or football showed they had much to learn about us. It truly was a two-way street.

Chapter 5

Whilst shopping for some groceries, a glance at the newspapers on sale revealed the date to be 25 August, meaning that nineteen days had elapsed this time. That knowledge reinforced the knowledge that visiting the Carnacans had improved my financial situation. By way of celebration, an expensive bottle of Margaux found its way into my basket.

A light lunch was followed by a short spell online catching up with local, national, and world news. I did not want to get caught unaware by not knowing about some major incident or development in the news during my stay within the barrier. Next, I stretched out on the sofa to ponder my situation. Assuming the Carnacans did not simplify matters by refusing further contact, I had decisions to make regarding how much normal human life I wanted in future. If future visits to Knocknashee were to be longer than those to date, there was a chance that friendships would come under strain. Entering inside the barrier rendered me incommunicado. My failure to respond to emails or text messages could be explained away only once, at most, twice. After that, no convincing explanation would be available. Similarly, a phone on the blink, preventing people from contacting me, could not be a regular feature. Even visits lasting just three weeks presented difficulties. I played bridge three nights a week. It would be easy enough to explain a couple of weeks' absence by inventing a trip abroad but, again, that would work only once or twice in the year. But, even if I were to stop playing bridge on a Friday and limit myself to just Monday and Tuesday, the five days I could be away equated to just two hours at slow-time speed. I found myself wondering if Mickey had experienced such problems.

Gradually, I formulated a provisional plan. I would not return to Knocknashee until Wednesday. This would enable me to play bridge on Monday or Tuesday of next week when I would inform my partners that I would be able to play only on alternate weeks. If pressed, I would explain that a close friend from Co Louth was keen to play with me more often as we were hoping to participate in international trials for the Irish team. As such, I would be playing in a Drogheda club on alternate Mondays and The Bankers in Dublin, where the standard was amongst the best in any club, on alternate Tuesdays. Friday night bridge would have to go, and I did not look forward to telling my partner, even though I intended to invent some course of study that would require my attendance in Dublin each Friday. These arrangements would allow me to spend twelve terrestrial days at a time at Knocknashee, which equated to over four hours at slow-time speed. It was far from ideal, but it would have to suffice.

Not returning there for nine days might have another benefit. It would show that I was not mad keen to get back inside the base. Indeed, Ixos and Citas might start to wonder whether I was going to return.

During the next few days, time seemed to drag, which I found rather ironic since it was passing sixty-four times quicker than I experienced at Knocknashee. As the hours dragged by, I found myself wondering about two topics. One concerned Ixos's reaction to my continuing absence. How would he interpret it? Did the fact that, by my intended return, only two hours would have elapsed inside the barrier alter his perception? The thought then struck me that there would, hopefully, be times when I would be returning to the base during their night-time, or did they experience night? I could not convince myself one way or the other, so I added it to the list of questions to be asked.

The second was the apparent lack of emotion displayed by Ixos and Citas. Neither seemed to have a sense of humour, neither displayed any anger and neither had any appreciation of the beauty of music. To them, it was simply an arrangement of sounds following mathematical patterns. Possibly linked to these traits was the story of the planned breeding programme on Carnac. Was sexual activity associated with passion and pleasure, or was it just a mechanical act necessary for procreation? Yet another question ...

Friday morning saw me reading the newspaper from cover to cover. As I was studying the bridge column, it occurred to me that deciding how a hand should be played was always easier when one could see all four hands. What if I used the thought-reading techniques I had learned from Ixos? If it worked, the game would become much easier, but would using the techniques be compliant with the laws of the game? After debating with myself, I reached the conclusion that it would be provided I did not read my partner's thoughts. The laws stipulate that communication between partners during the auction and play shall be affected only by means of calls and plays. Reading my partner's thoughts would breach that law but reading my opponents' thoughts would not. The laws did not contain any prohibition regarding mind reading. Indeed, they expressly permitted deductions based on observations of opponents' mannerisms. I was aware that my reasoning was rather Jesuitical. After all, if I knew what cards each opponent held, I would know what my partner held. I dismissed this mental objection by reasoning that different players possessed different skills and abilities. Some had excellent memories, enabling them to remember complex bidding systems and what cards had been played. Others had logical minds, allowing them to read the situation at any stage during play. Yet, others had, for want of a better term, great "card sense." Some had all three. Surely, my recently acquired ability fell into a similar category. Perhaps some of the top players against whom I had competed also possessed such ability without broadcasting the fact.

On Monday night, my ability to read my opponents' thoughts proved advantageous in around one-quarter of the hands we played. For most of the rest, it had no effect as I would have bid and played in the same way anyway. With one hand, it seemed to steer me in the wrong direction entirely. Our opponents had bid game in spades, and the cards I knew them to hold would enable declarer to make his contract. He would lose one trick in spades, one in hearts and one in diamonds but, having a void, would not lose any in clubs. This knowledge prompted me to bid on in clubs as a sacrifice, calculating that going down by three tricks, presumably doubled, which I was, would be preferable to allowing our opponents to make their vulnerable game. As it happened, I went down by only two tricks. It should have been three, but one opponent revoked meaning that one of their tricks was transferred to me. The revoke occurred because he had the five of clubs sorted in amongst his spade holding. It followed that he would have lost a club as well as the other three tricks thereby going down in his spade contract. I did see the funny side of it but could not share the joke with anyone.

Perhaps understandably, I found that much of the pleasure had disappeared from the game. It no longer presented any real challenge. So, it proved to be an easy decision to abandon thought-reading during bridge – club bridge anyway. I was not so sure that I would be able to resist using it during national competitions or international trials.

Wednesday morning arrived at last, and, having packed my picnic, I headed for Knocknashee. Scarcely had I sat down on the usual rock when the entrance to underground opened, and Ixos came out. His expression was inscrutable, so it was impossible to judge what the decision from Carnac was, if indeed he had received any decision. It was with immense relief that I heard the words, "Welcome back. I can impart to you our observations on humanity. I hope you feel able to answer some more of our questions."

I replied that I would do my best but added that I had a request to make before we started. I pointed out that whenever he or Citas answered my questions, the answer given had just the minimum amount of information, thereby necessitating further questions. Would it not be preferable if they volunteered all information that might be relevant? Ixos replied that such an approach would require them to guess what I wanted to know. There was little point in them giving me a lot of information I might not want. It would be preferable to stick with the process whereby they answered direct questions. I could see that persuading him to alter his approach would be difficult indeed, so I did not pursue the matter.

Ixos accepted without demur my statement that I needed to restrict my visit to just over four hours. He agreed to remind me whenever the four-hour-long period was ending to ensure I departed on time. We entered underground and began this visit's exchange of information.

When Carnacan explorers first observed humans, they were uncertain as to whether they were seeing one species or several. On Carnac, the height of almost all adults was within a range of about four inches. With humans, the range of heights of those who appeared to be adult was in excess of twenty-five inches. There was also the great variety in skin pigmentation in humans. All Carnacans shared a pale complexion whereas, with humans, some were very pale pink, others differing shades of brown and yet others differing shades of black. The matter was the subject of much debate among Carnacan scientists.

It was only whenever the humans were brought to Carnac that the question was resolved, and the answer surprised the scientists. During the journey and prior to the various tests and ultimate dissection, the humans were kept under close observation. It had been noted that only two out of the ten seemed able to understand one another, which lent support to the school of thought that several species existed. But the scientific results were unequivocal; despite all appearances, there was just one human species or, to be more precise, all ten of the specimens brought to Carnac were of the same species.

So, the observation bases were set up and the study of humanity began. At the conclusion of their tour, the crews transported copies of all recordings to Carnac. They also prepared detailed reports that outlined the progress made on deciphering human language and observations on various aspects of human behaviour.

One aspect of human behaviour was the cause of much concern amongst Carnacan scientists: aggression. Instances of aggressive behaviour were not unknown on Carnac but were very rare. Any that did occur were investigated, and, in every case, the Carnacan involved was found to have either suffered a head injury or developed a tumour affecting the brain. Undoubtedly, some of the instances witnessed with humans would have been due to similar causes but the frequency of instances of aggressive behaviour rendered it most unlikely that all of it could be attributed to illness or injury.

Episodes involving aggression took various forms. At times, the aggression was purely verbal, or it might be accompanied by threatening gestures. On other occasions, the aggressor employed violence often using some sort of weapon, which could result in injury or even the demise of the other human. Often the non-aggressor appeared to submit to the will of the aggressor but that was far from a universal reaction. Many instances were observed where the other person became just as aggressive as the original aggressor, often leading to combat between the two parties.

Carnacan scientists were puzzled by this aggression. Normal behaviour for Carnacans is to act in a way that promotes the greater good. This involves cooperation with others. Aggression has no part to play in Carnacan society. Violence was only used on those rare occasions when it was necessary to defend oneself, or other Carnacans, against attack by another species. My protest that aggression and violence against the person were forbidden in human society only served to increase Ixos's puzzlement. "If humanity does not want aggression and violence, why do so many humans employ aggression and violence?" he asked. However much I sought to convince him that the great majority of humanity was essentially peaceable and non-aggressive, he remained unconvinced. From his viewpoint, the number of humans who engaged in aggression or violence had him, and many other Carnacans, wondering as to the cause of this phenomenon and whether the situation could ever be remedied.

Even more puzzling to Carnacans were the episodes where one group of humans would attack another group. During the early periods of observation, such groups were comparatively small, rarely exceeding a few thousand in number. For the most part, these groups met in combat in open spaces, and the conflict often resulted in the death or serious injury of up to one-third of the combatants on either side. On occasion, two groups would engage in a series of battles within a short period of time. There were other episodes where a group would attack a human settlement. The attack might involve surrounding the settlement for a long period of time during which neither humans nor any type of goods, including food, were permitted to enter or leave the settlement. It appeared that the aim was to deprive the occupants of food, leading to death by starvation. On some occasions, the settlement was captured more or less undamaged but often it was destroyed with fire, the most common method of destruction.

In more recent times, the nature of combat seems to have changed. Initially, it was just an increase of the numbers involved. France's invasion of Russia in the early nineteenth century was undertaken by a massive army. But this paled into insignificance when compared to the number of participants in the conflict that convulsed Europe between 1914 and 1918. Millions took part on either side, and millions perished or were left with life-changing injuries. That conflict also showed the changing nature of conflict. It was the first truly mechanised war. It featured much heavy artillery. Vehicles made of steel, which offered some protection to the occupants, were used by both sides. These vehicles carried a large piece of artillery and their use brought about the possibility of fast-moving conflict. Even the still-primitive aircraft then available were pressed into military service. But despite this mechanisation, it was essentially a static conflict with huge numbers facing each other a short distance apart, bombarding each other's positions. It was not just artillery used in those bombardments. Both sides seemed to strive to introduce new ways of killing their opponents. Flamethrowers were used as was poison gas. It was a truly horrendous conflict.

The observers in the various bases thought that they had witnessed conflict at its worst. However, just over two decades later, they realised they could not have been more wrong in that belief. The conflict lasting from 1939 to 1945 brought about not just loss of life on an unbelievable scale but the systematic destruction of many human settlements. It seemed irrelevant to those doing the killing, or carrying out the destruction, that many of those affected were not engaged in the conflict. The ultimate acts of killing and destruction took place in Japan just days prior to the cessation of hostilities.

After the end of hostilities in Europe came the discovery that one party to the conflict had systematically killed around six million people, many of them citizens of that country.

The events of those two major conflicts had led many observers and scientists back on Carnac to question the wisdom of continuing to assess humanity as a possible addition to Carnac's genetic pool. Such aggressive and destructive behaviour surely rendered humanity quite unsuitable for that role. It was likely that any Carnacan-human offspring would display similar traits. Society on Carnac could not be exposed to such a risk.

After much deliberation, the decision was taken to continue the humanity project. A number of factors influenced that decision. Firstly, aggressive behaviour apart, humanity appeared to be more suitable than either of the other two species the Carnacans considered. Human science, technology and medical knowledge had developed much more quickly than on either of the other planets where society, although peaceful, was still very primitive. On one planet, the wheel had not been invented. Secondly, it was hoped that medical advances might make available some method of removing the aggressive trait displayed by humanity. Finally, humanity's aggressive behaviour was so far removed from normal Carnacan experience that scientists felt it merited further study. After all, the observers were already in place, so continuing the project was pretty much cost free.

"You can play a big part in this project," declared Ixos. "We think that obtaining a human perspective on aggression and conflict will contribute significantly to our understanding of the matter. We are also conscious of other areas where our knowledge and understanding is extremely limited. Furthermore, there may be other areas of human behaviour where we don't even know there are gaps in our knowledge. Therefore, we will answer any questions you ask about our observations on humanity. We hope you will feel equally free to answer all of our questions to the best of your knowledge." I suddenly felt almost overwhelmed by the situation. My contribution to the Carnacan study of humanity potentially could make a difference to the future of two different planets. I replied that I was grateful for their decision and would do my best to reciprocate.

So began a series of conversations not just with Ixos and Citas but with all their companions at the base. Except for Ixos, who took a broad overview, each of the crew focussed their attention on one particular area of human behaviour. Over time, I became able to tell them apart using minor physical differences, but I noted that each Carnacan's temperament and general demeanour was indistinguishable from the others. On some visits, I spent the entire four hours with a single Carnacan. On others, my time was split between two or three of them. In some areas, I was impressed with the extent of their knowledge, but with others, I was amazed at how little they knew. Sometimes their misunderstanding was almost comical.

I found the whole process mentally exhausting and was glad for the two-day rest back in Newry between conversations. Sometimes the break enabled me to reflect further on a topic we had discussed. It could be a disconcerting experience to look in detail at an area of human behaviour one had never previously considered in any depth. But it was absolutely necessary to learn more about Carnacan behaviour and society.

The first topic the Carnacans wished to discuss was human aggression and violence. This was not unexpected as this area was the source of their real concern about the suitability of humanity as breeding partners. The commencement of my conversation with Magas was direct, to say the least. "Have you ever been aggressive towards or employed violence against another human?" he asked. Realising that I had to be totally honest, I told him that I had been aggressive on a few occasions and had employed violence on two occasions. He expressed surprise at my answer, saying that I seemed to be a very calm and peaceable person. I explained that all of the incidents had been during my childhood and that fights between children, which seldom resulted in serious hurt, were not viewed as serious.

"So, why do you think are humans aggressive? Why do they employ violence?" was his next question. My reply seemed to do little to aid his comprehension. I outlined various reasons including the taking of offence, defending or coveting property, competition between males for the attention of a female, gang violence and intoxication or drug use. Magas expressed his lack of understanding and suggested that we looked at each reason in depth. He was quite open in stating that none of those reasons were within Carnacan experience.

Magas struggled to grasp the concept of taking offence. From his viewpoint, every person was entitled to hold any opinion on any topic and was similarly entitled to express that viewpoint. The fact that another person might hold and express a different opinion should not present any difficulty. Each should recognise the right of the other to hold and express whatever opinion they wished. "But what if the opinion expressed by one person insulted the other or was in any way derogatory?" I asked. Magas said that he had never witnessed such a happening on Carnac but that he did not think it should cause any problem. I sought to explain the concept of ego, but that left Magas mystified. "Why should any person think that their opinion is more important than that of any other person? Why should any person think their opinions or actions are beyond the critical review of others?" he asked. We spent a long time on this topic, and I still was not convinced he fully understood human egotism or the taking or giving of offence.

The defence or coveting of property was initially even more incomprehensible to him. "What do you mean by property?" he asked. Initially, I tried to explain that people owned land, a house, a business or goods and felt entitled to take whatever action was necessary to retain that ownership. By contrast, some others might wish to acquire that land, etc. without paying for it. "Own? What do you mean?" was the question repeated by Magas. Slowly, it dawned on me that he really did not have any comprehension of the concept of ownership, so I changed tack by asking him about land, housing, furniture, vehicles, etc. on Carnac. Given Magas's incomprehension of ownership, it came as no surprise to learn that no Carnacan possessed any property or goods. Housing was constructed by those with the relevant skills to meet perceived need. Similarly, furniture, such as tables, chairs, and beds were made in whatever quantity was required. Crops were grown and livestock raised on the same basis. Each Carnacan had sufficient supplies to meet his or her needs. Housing was all of similar size unlike that on Earth. Here, the Carnacans had been puzzled to discover that a very few dwelt in large mansions. A larger number lived in houses which, though smaller than the mansions, were much larger than was actually required. On the other hand, many lived in very cramped accommodation, which was quite clearly inadequate for the number of occupants, and some seemed to lack any accommodation. Eventually, Magas reached an understanding of the concept of ownership but expressed his opinion that it offered no advantages to the Carnacan system. On the contrary, he could see serious disadvantages.

I wished to hear his views on those disadvantages but first sought information on decision making processes on Carnac. Administrators are selected at random I was informed. Decisions on routine matters such as how many dwellings to build or what crops to grow on any piece of land are made by these administrators at the regional level. Each region contains around 100 million people. Where specialist knowledge is required, persons with the relevant knowledge or skills are appointed, again at random, to advise the administrators. Administrators and their specialist advisors serve for four years.

From each region, one person is selected at random to serve as an administrator or decisions on matters of planet-wide importance. Such matters include the space exploration programme and major scientific projects. Again, they are advised by the relevant experts chosen at random. The development of the time dilator, development of part particle, part energy stuff and decisions on which areas existed at which time speeds are examples of matters whereby decisions were made by these administrators on behalf of the entire planet.

Various questions came to mind as I absorbed this information, but I thought it better to give Carnacan administration more thought before discussing it further. Besides, Magas told me that Ixos had a much greater knowledge of the topic than he.

We returned to the question of private ownership, and Magas outlined his views. It was a very inefficient method of utilising resources and providing for the needs of the population. What was the sense in two people occupying a dwelling covering 6,000 or 7,000 square feet? Surely, 1,000 square feet would be more than adequate for their genuine needs. That meant that other living space had to be provided elsewhere for around a dozen people. Similarly, one person having sole control over a large tract of land meant that the needs or best interest of other humans were often ignored. The situation regarding scientific discoveries and technology was even more problematic. Whereas, on Carnac, all scientific and technological advances were shared openly, humans acted in ways to keep them secret from some. Magas and his companions had been puzzled by this behaviour because it seemed counterproductive to the interests of humanity. Now Magas had some understanding of why it happened but still thought it very short-sighted. "Do you think we could have developed the time dilator, or the stuff for the barrier, if each scientist who made any sort of advance tried to keep that knowledge to himself?" he asked. I attempted to explain that potential future profit was often cited as the driving force behind research undertaken by individuals or companies. I had to digress into a description of companies. Magas was far from convinced. He described various examples of technology that had been improved much more slowly than it might have been because it was owned by one person or company. I had to laugh when he used a human proverb to reinforce his arguments. "Many hands make light work," he declared. "And many minds make light work better!" I had no answer to that one.

We would return to the topic of private ownership on many occasions. After aggression and violence, it was the aspect of human behaviour that puzzled Carnacans the most. Even those investigating other topics tended to stray into this area. I could understand their curiosity. Any human studying behaviour on Carnac would struggle to come to terms with the absence of private ownership. Additionally, knowing about private ownership enabled the Carnacans to begin to understand properly many things that had seemed inexplicable. One of those things had been the round pieces of metal humans often passed to another human who had given them goods. In more recent times, pieces of paper were often used instead of, or alongside, the metal pieces. It took a while, but I managed to educate Magas and the others about money. Citas appeared to grasp the concept better than any of the others. He could see that, whilst one item might be equivalent in value to another item, carrying that item around in the hope that some person owning the other item might want to swap could be awkward, especially if the item were bulky. Having something that was readily portable and universally accepted as an alternative to actual goods was pretty much a necessity if commerce was to thrive. He further displayed his understanding by enquiring into who controlled the production of notes and coinage and was especially interested in the question of counterfeit money. During a couple of conversations, he showed that he also understood such topics as simple and compound interest, profit and loss accounting, stocks and shares, government bonds and taxation. As a former Inspector of Taxes, these topics were familiar to me, but I was amazed when Citas displayed a greater knowledge and understanding than many of my former colleagues.

However, I was able to surprise him when we got around to discussing the value humanity might put on, for want of a better term, Carnacan possessions. He readily understood that the stuff of which the barrier was composed, or a time dilator, would be valued very highly by humans. Similarly, sub-ethereal transmitters and receivers or some of their medication would be highly valued by humans. But Citas was absolutely flabbergasted when I told him that some of their recording archive would attract extremely high values if offered to humanity. With his assistance, I located the following examples. Starting locally, footage of the Battle of the Boyne would be of great interest not just to historians but also the Orange Order. I had to give him a brief resume of Irish history. Next, I drew his attention to footage of another battle, this time in 1066, which included coverage of the fatal injury suffered by Harold. The significance of the Battle of Hastings in British history cannot be overstated, and the footage was best described, by that overused term, as priceless. Similar considerations applied to footage of the storming of the Bastille, Mark Anthony's funeral oration for Julius Caesar, the combat between Achilles and Hector, and Hannibal's elephants descending from Alpine passes. It struck me as ironic in the extreme that the Carnacans possessed archive footage which, if put up for sale, would command prices in the millions, if not billions, of pounds, euros or dollars. Yet however much money the footage could realise, it would be of absolutely no value to the Carnacans. Indeed, given that selling the footage would reveal the Carnacan presence on Earth, it would effectively bring an end to the observation process. Once humanity became aware of the observation process, that awareness could modify human behaviour, rendering any conclusions invalid.

Explaining men competing for the attention of a woman proved to be a very difficult task. It was also somewhat embarrassing because Magas brought Jamil, one of female crew, into the discussion. Very quickly, it became obvious that neither had any comprehension of sexual attraction. Before embarking on a lesson describing human sexual activity, I asked them to outline what happened on Carnac if a male and female wished to produce a child. Jamil reminded me of the breeding programme that existed on their home planet. Administrators decided who should breed with whom. At the appropriate time during the female's menstrual cycle, the two had sexual intercourse. Fertilisation in that way was considered preferable to the alternative of in-vitro fertilisation. Sexual intercourse was regarded as a simple mechanical process whereby the male's sperm was introduced into the female's vagina. The male brought about an erection by thought processes and caused ejaculation in the same way. His penis would be inside the female for less than a minute. All this was done in a calm manner.

Describing and explaining human sexual activity to Magas and Jamil was more difficult than giving a sex education class to eleven- and twelve-year-olds. Even before puberty, young humans are familiar with familial love. They might not have experienced sexual attraction or urges, but they have experienced various emotions. By contrast, the Carnacans seemed devoid of any emotional feelings and found it difficult to comprehend sexual attraction. Sexual urges and orgasms were quite beyond the scope of their imagination. I tried to describe how it felt when one found a woman sexually attractive. Then, I endeavoured to outline how one felt when sexually aroused. Jamil's presence certainly did not make this process any easier. I do not know if any writer has ever been totally successful in describing orgasm, and I am sure my attempts did little to enlighten Magas and Jamil. They were both very interested when I related how a couple might embark on foreplay before sexual intercourse. I described how each might explore their partner's body with hands, lips and tongue. Embarrassing as I found it, I described in full detail cunnilingus and fellatio. I thought Magas was displaying a rare flash of humour when he suggested that they might obtain a better understanding by way of a practical demonstration and that Jamil would be a suitable partner for me for that. Now, taking Jamil to bed would certainly not be an unpleasant task. Around five feet tall, she was stunningly beautiful with a terrific figure. I could scarcely believe it when she indicated that she agreed with Magas. From her perspective, it would be a valid scientific experiment – a unique opportunity to study human sexuality from close up. Both she and I would wear bracelets to monitor our heart rates, blood pressure and respiration. A microchip injected into each of us would record the levels of various hormones in our circulations.

Initially, Magas wished to be in the room as an observer but acceded to my request that Jamil and I be on our own in the room. I explained that, for humans, sexual activity was considered to be something that should be done in private and that having another present might impact on my enjoyment thus altering the readings they might obtain from the bracelet and microchip. Magas did persuade me to allow him to instal a camera in the room so that he might observe remotely.

It had been a couple of decades since I had engaged in sexual activity with a woman of Jamil's age and beauty, and I was worried that the great sexual excitement I felt as we stripped each other naked might lead to premature ejaculation. I need not have worried. As I embarked on foreplay, I found Jamil willing to engage in anything I suggested but lacking in the bodily responses one would have expected from a human. It was slightly disconcerting although it did not prevent me from enjoying a very satisfactory orgasm. As I came, the thought entered my mind: "Lie back and think of Carnac!"

When we had dressed and rejoined Magas, he said that the readings from the bracelet gave him some understanding why humans were so keen to engage in sexual activity that they were prepared to resort to violence to see off others whom they perceived as rivals. My respiration, pulse and blood pressure had not just been increasingly elevated as the sexual activity progressed but had peaked as I experienced orgasm. By contrast, Jamil's readings had remained normal throughout. It was too early to comment on the hormonal activity, but Magas would expect to see elevated levels of testosterone and endorphins with a real spike in the latter at orgasm. During my next visit, he confirmed that the readings transmitted by the microchip corresponded with his expectations. As had been expected, Jamil's hormonal levels had been unaffected by the sexual activity.

I was somewhat alarmed when Magas said they had footage of what seemed to be sexual activity involving persons of the same sex. I found myself describing what I knew about homosexual practices. Before Magas could suggest any experimentation, I stated that this was not something I was prepared to demonstrate.

I switched the emphasis back to Carnac by enquiring whether they had anything akin to marriage. They do not. Children live with their mothers, and most have little or no contact with their biological fathers. Children are regarded as children of society, not just of one couple. Next, I asked about a potential paradoxical situation. Suppose a couple, both aged thirty, produce a child. The father continues living at one sixty-fourth-time speed, but the mother and child move to a normal-time-speed region. By the time the father is thirty-two, the child will be 128 years old – four times older than his father. Magas said that it was likely such a situation had occurred on occasion but was keen to emphasise that the apparent paradox was illusory. The child was just living his life at a faster speed.

Gang violence proved much easier for Magas to understand. He quickly grasped that gangs were essentially a scaled down version of countries or tribes. This, and his newfound understanding of private possession, enabled him to understand the actions of those gangs who were engaged in robbery. He surprised me by stating that such gangs were neither a modern phenomenon nor a purely urban one. Magas cited the Border Reivers as one example. He could also understand those who were involved in the distribution and sale of illegal substances, such as heroin, cocaine or cannabis. Again, he was aware of historical precedents, such as mafia activity during prohibition in the US. What did puzzle him were the activities of gangs who appeared to engage in violence with no apparent motive. This time, the historic precedent was comparatively recent – Mods and Rockers. I sought to explain that some groups were simply intolerant of those who were in any way different to them. Such differences might be skin colour, hair style or dress code. Often, the gang members were of limited intelligence and had little educational attainment. Other gangs were essentially territorial. Typically, they all lived in one locality and regarded those living in any neighbouring locality as enemies. We spent quite a while discussing territorial gangs without Magas understanding how or why one person could hate another to such an extent that they resorted to violence.

Neither could he, needless to say, comprehend xenophobia. Whilst he could see that those of one skin colour might feel different to, and distrustful of, those of a different colour, he simply could not understand why the various countries of Europe had been at each other's throats on so many occasions down through the centuries. Did humans not realise that conflict was to the detriment of all parties involved whilst cooperation always benefited everyone? This was a topic to which we returned frequently.

Both intoxication through consumption of alcohol and self-incapacitation through use of various drugs had Magas absolutely bewildered. Why would any person set out to reduce their ability to think clearly? Why would any person risk the severe illness and physical harm associated with overconsumption of alcohol or drug use, especially via intravenous injection? Why risk a permanent reduction in their intellectual capacity? What made the matter even more incomprehensible were the after-effects of drunkenness. Nausea, intestinal problems, and cephalalgia appeared to be universally recognised as likely to occur after drunkenness, yet people still persisted in becoming intoxicated. Similarly, withdrawal symptoms from heroin use were well-known yet people continued to inject. My description of addiction went a little way to enlightening him, but he argued that since various substances were known to be addictive, those who embarked on their use were acting totally irrationally.

Whilst we were discussing drugs, Magas asked about the small thin cylinders which people lit and put to their lips. The burning cylinders produced smoke, which people appeared to inhale. What was the rationale behind this? His chief difficulty was the obvious potential for serious damage to the lungs and circulation. I told him that his concerns were well-founded, and I outlined the enormous numbers of lung cancer victims throughout the world in any country where smoking became fashionable. Add in victims of emphysema and heart disease, and the true cost to humanity of smoking was revealed. Again, his puzzlement was reduced only slightly when I informed him of the very addictive nature of nicotine. "If people are aware of the health risks from smoking and aware of the addictiveness of nicotine, why do they start?" he asked. I was unable to offer any sensible answer.

Chapter 6

Among the most enjoyable conversations were those I had with Besil. She specialised in linguistics. Besil recounted the problems encountered by the first observers in translating human speech into their own tongue. With nobody to guide them, their initial efforts were very much hit and miss. What they tried to do was to identify situations where one person appeared to be giving instructions to another. Most frequently, it would be an adult speaking to a juvenile. The actions of the juvenile would be monitored following receipt of the instruction. Use of this method, supported by some very powerful computers, enabled the first breakthroughs to be made. After that, the task became somewhat easier. The more they knew about human speech, the simpler it became to translate further words.

The earliest success had come at a base in southern Europe. This was shared with other bases. Thus was revealed the scale of the task. Only one of the other bases could recognise any of the language that had been translated. They realised that humans used a multiplicity of languages, some of which bore similarities to others whilst others were quite radically different. No wonder those humans who had been taken to Carnac had been unable to communicate with each other.

Even with the many human languages requiring translation, very few linguists found themselves working in total isolation. Generally, there were at least two bases working on any tongue. The linguists would share any progress with all other bases working on that language or any language that appeared to be closely related. Those linguists arriving in replacement crews studied previous progress both prior to departing Carnac and during the journey. But Besil's experience showed that such preparations were not guaranteed to be sufficient.

During the greater part of her predecessor's stay, almost all of the population of Ireland spoke the same language, Gaelic.

Besil herself had acquired a good working knowledge of that tongue. But, over time, things had changed. Even before her arrival, it had been noted that a sizeable number of people from the neighbouring island had moved to Ireland, mostly to the northern part of the island. These people spoke a different language. Gradually, this other language, English, supplanted Gaelic as the vernacular until, by the start of the twentieth century, Gaelic was used in everyday speech only in a few small, mostly rural, areas. As a consequence, Besil was required to learn English as well. Whilst she was the specialist linguist, the need to have some knowledge initially of Gaelic, but latterly of English, applied to all at the base.

Her companions in various bases in England were of considerable assistance to Besil in her study of English. However, she soon discovered significant variations between the English spoken in England and that used in Ireland. This had puzzled her. Back on Carnac, all spoke the same language, and all used it in the same way. No matter where on the planet one lived, every word had the same meaning and was pronounced in the same way. This did not appear to be the case on Earth. Not only were there many different languages but each language seemed to have a number of different versions. "Did humans really want to communicate with each other?" she asked.

I could understand her bewilderment. I was accustomed to the different versions of spoken English. One did not have to be a skilled linguist to be able to recognise regional dialects. Nor did one need a very sensitive ear to distinguish between different accents. One of my teachers at school could place to within a few miles the area in which any person had been raised by listening to them speak for just a couple of minutes. But if one was raised on a planet where the spoken language was totally uniform, such variations must seem strange. It would be akin to somebody who had only ever heard BBC English spoken with a refined home counties accent first hearing a south-western dialect spoken with a soft Devonian burr or a broad Belfast accent.

I did my best to explain how regional dialects had come into being. I recounted how, up until the advent of rail travel and later the motor car, the great majority of people did not travel far from their home. If followed, there was insufficient social mixing between regions to maintain a uniform language. Over time, minor variations developed which, over the centuries, became sufficient to create problems for a person from one region conversing with one from another. This problem did not affect written language, but, since only a small minority was literate until education became more widespread during the nineteenth century, the existence of a more standardised written language did little to prevent the development of regional dialects. The differences between various dialects were exacerbated by the development of differences in pronunciation.

Besil sought my assistance in understanding some recordings that had puzzled her companions and her. "Are you looking for a dig in the beak (pronounced bake)?" was one of them. Besil thought that dig meant to turn over soil and "bake" meant to cook something. She had tried constructions, but none made any sort of sense, not that human behaviour or speech were guaranteed to be sensible. She shook her head in disbelief when I said, "Do you want a punch in the mouth?" "How can that be the case?" she asked. Thus began a long chat on the use of slang. I explained that dig was a slang term for punch, and beak was one for mouth. The fact that Frankies pronounced the word as bake was an added complication. "Now I am even more confused," Besil said. "I would have thought Frankies lived in France, but the recording was made in Belfast." It had been rather mischievous of me to use the term Frankies, but I had been unable to resist the temptation. So, I recounted the story of the evacuation of many Belfast residents in the aftermath of the Belfast blitz. Food rationing was in force during the war, and initially there were problems in providing all the evacuees with the relevant ration books. As a temporary measure, following issue of the foodstuffs to which they were entitled, their hands were marked, or franked, using a rubber stamp and inkpad. The nickname stuck.

I was able to help explain various other terms that had puzzled Besil and her companions. "Your head's a marley" was one such term. She was aware that marley was commonly used instead of marble when talking about the small, coloured glass balls with which children played. But she was unable to deduce any sensible meaning for the phrase that featured in many recordings. I had to admit that, whilst I could tell her it meant "You are talking nonsense," I had no idea how it originated.

I laughed when I heard that Belfast classic, "Do you think I came up the Lagan in a bubble?" Besil struggled to understand how this could be translated into "Do you think I am gullible?" Once more, I could not explain the origins of the expression. I could only point to that quirky sense of humour found in Belfast. This was of no help whatsoever given that Carnacans had no concept of humour.

"Up shit creek without a paddle" was another. I told Besil that this was one that did not originate in Northern Ireland but was widely used throughout the UK. I also informed her that there existed related phrases, such as "in deep shit" and "in deep doo-doo". All meant "in real trouble." Once I explained that being immersed in human excrement would be a most unpleasant experience, Besil was able to comprehend the use of such phrases although she had difficulties with understanding why people did not speak in a more straightforward fashion. My explanations for "quare geg," "face like a smacked arse," "away with the fairies," and "in Stubb's" merely served to confirm her suspicions that human dialogue was not really designed to enlighten the listener.

Nor did another explanation of mine reduce those suspicions. She pointed out that, up until the 1980s, there had been very few non-white people in Ireland. Yet there were many recordings where people had been called "black bastard," often in an aggressive manner. Explaining the intertwined political and religious divides that exist in Northern Ireland can be difficult enough when one is addressing an English person, rendering them comprehensible to a non-human was an even more arduous task.

Eventually, Besil came to the core of the problem. Many English words had two or more meanings, which were, in many instances, remarkably disparate. The list was endless. Can, lark, moor, plot, trip, and burn were just a few of the words we discussed. Just as confusing were the many examples of words which, though different, sounded the same. Sew, sow, and so, peel, and peal, boar and bore, and plum and plumb took a little time to explain.

Just as problematic was the way in which some words acquired a different meaning over time. Fit was one example. Originally, it referred just to physical fitness but, during the previous twenty years, it came to be used to indicate physical attractiveness. Cool was another. For centuries, it referred to comparative temperature but, in the sixties, was used as synonym for good or desirable. I found it amusing that Besil had chosen this example because cool itself had, temporarily at least, acquired an alter ego. The predictive text feature on mobile phones tended to bring up book, instead of cool, leading to the use of book instead of cool especially among the student population.

Following our first conversation, Besil must have been in contact with other bases in English-speaking areas because she asked for explanations of several phrases, all of which involved Cockney rhyming slang. When she asked what "My plates were killing me" meant, I rather naughtily just stated, "I had sore feet." To her credit, she tried to decipher the link between the phrase and its meaning. After a while, I relented and told her "plates" was just the first part of "plates of meat" and explained the concept of rhyme. Even knowing about rhyming slang, Besil could not see the link between "Brahms and List" and intoxication until I told her that "pissed" was slang for drunk. Perhaps the most ridiculous recording I was asked to interpret was: "Such Bristols, I could hardly Adam and Eve my mince pies!" However, I was delighted when I was not required to explain it all. After I had gone through the link from Bristols, through Bristol Cities and then the slang term titties, to breasts and explained that Adam and Eve rhymed with believe, Besil said that mince pies must mean eyes. Clearly, my tutorials were of some benefit.

On one occasion, I just could not resist the temptation to fabricate an explanation. The phrase was "He drew the short straw." I invented a pagan religious sect who worshipped straw as a bearer of life-giving food. Its adherents would draw a short straw, which they used as an aid to contemplation. Besil duly conveyed this bum explanation to her colleague in England. When I corrected the explanation during my next visit, I expected Besil to be annoyed. Instead, she just said that she would inform her colleague.

During our conversations it emerged that the Carnacans had only very limited access to written language on earth. Not having access to the interior of any building, they had been confined to studying inscriptions on monuments, later on road signs, posters, signs in shop windows, and road signs. None of these contained a sufficiently large sample of written language to enable any progress to be made in deciphering it. Besil asked if I could bring some examples of written English on my next visit and if I would teach her how to read it. I was delighted to agree to her request.

What does one use to teach written English to an alien? After some thought, I decided that one needed examples that were well written, grammatically correct and properly punctuated. Clearly, some of the classics were required. So, I raided my modest personal library and visited a couple of second-hand bookshops. My selections included *The Old Curiosity Shop, War and Peace, The Brothers Karamazov, Animal Farm, Anne of Green Gables, Scoop, To Kill A Mockingbird* and *For Whom The Bell Tolls*. I added in Walton's *Golden Treasury of Poetry*. By way of factual writing, I resurrected my half-century-old chemistry textbook by Morrison and Boyd. I thought it would do no harm to ascertain what the Carnacans thought of human knowledge of chemistry. Truly contemporary writing was represented by recent copies of *The Times, The Guardian* and *The Telegraph* newspapers.

I anticipated that teaching written English would not be easy. The potential problems included the lack of a regular grammatical structure and the rather irregular spelling. One thing in my favour was that Besil and the others had a decent knowledge of spoken English. Most teachers have to teach written and spoken English side by side. I would not have to do that.

Lessons progressed slowly at first, but Besil surprised me by the facility with which she conquered various aspects of the language. She was aided by a phenomenal memory allied to a quite brilliant intellect. At the end of our sixth lesson, she indicated a wish to assist her counterparts in other bases to learn written English. For this to happen, she needed my assistance. What she would like was for each base to have a copy of each of five books. That would enable the linguist and others to participate in lessons by way of remote learning. She would like me to accompany her on a few trips to deliver the books. This would require me to be away from my home for longer than my current visits. The journey to even the other base in Ireland, which was near Carlow town, would require almost three hours in each direction. Add in that she would like me to give one face-to-face lesson at the base, and one was at least doubling the length of my absence. If necessary, she could deliver the books without me, but she thought it preferable that I accompany her. She added that her counterparts were very keen to meet the sole human with whom Carnacans had currently any contact.

This request found me undecided, and I asked for time to think about it. Collating the sets of books would be the easy part. Being away from home for extended periods would be more problematic. Currently, I literally, as well as figuratively, enjoyed the best of both worlds. That happy situation would come to an end if I agreed to Besil's request. I would be throwing in my lot with the Carnacan's and effectively abandoning my friendships with several people. Was I prepared to do that? Conversely, was I prepared to forgo the opportunity to travel in an invisible vehicle both through Ireland and across to mainland UK? Neither was a choice I wanted to make but choose I must.

The matter scarcely left my thoughts during my next visit home to the extent that my mind was far from bidding and play during bridge on Tuesday night. My performance was so poor that my partner solicitously enquired as to my health. He was convinced that I must have been ill. Indeed, my distracted state almost brought about my demise when I stepped out in front of traffic. By the time I was setting out again for Knocknashee, I had reached what I thought was a compromise solution. I would travel to the base near Carlow whenever Besil was ready to go, but I would not travel to any other base for at least a further six terrestrial months. Any later trip would need to be short enough so that I was away from Newry for no more than a month or so.

The journey to Knocknashee was not as straightforward than usual. Normally, I walked the entire three miles. But this time, I was burdened with eight sets of five books, which proved quite heavy. This was half the number I had obtained during my visit home. I had resorted to buying them new because sourcing so many secondhand books would have been nigh on impossible. Additionally, I was carrying a couple of changes of shirts, underwear and socks and some toiletries. I had considered taking a taxi the whole way but decided that being dropped off with luggage in the middle of nowhere would attract suspicion. So, I picked a house, whose owner I knew, which lay just over a quarter of a mile away from the base. Under normal circumstances, he and his wife would be at work, and I just hoped neither of them would be enjoying a day off. I knew they never locked the garden shed, which would enable me to leave part of my burden in it and make two trips to the base. Even so, the taxi driver looked askance at me but, fortunately, did not ask any questions.

Besil and Ixos were as inscrutable as ever when I announced my decision. Both stated that it was understandable although they hoped that, at some stage, I would change my mind. When I asked when Besil wished us to travel to Carlow, she replied, "As soon as possible." Ixos indicated that preparing the vehicle for such a long journey would take almost two hours. They had not commenced that process because they had not known what my decision would be. I asked why the journey would take almost three hours when the vehicle was capable of covering the distance in little more than an hour. He explained that the slower journey was very much a precautionary measure. Whilst the vehicle was totally invisible, they had no guarantee that it was indetectable. Indeed, they suspected that some human technology registered faint traces of the vehicles. Such traces were more likely when the vehicle was travelling at high speed. Additionally, there were safety considerations. Not only was the vehicle invisible but also silent. Furthermore, the vehicle did not employ anything akin to headlights. Looking out through the front was akin to using night vision equipment. The Carnacans did not wish to put humans at risk from being struck without warning by a vehicle travelling at a hundred miles per hour. The Carnacans were excellent drivers, but their abilities still suffered limitations. Whilst their reaction times were better than their human counterparts, reaction was not instantaneous. For this reason, speeds in excess of forty-five miles per hour were not used unless in emergency.

Two hours later, having watched the vehicle being prepared and cargo stowed, Besil and I sat in our seats waiting to be informed that the barrier would permit our exit. I felt strangely calm. It was akin to waiting for a plane to start taxiing down the runway. Of course, I was aware that I was one of only a handful of humans to have ever sat in such a vehicle and, because Mickey had never travelled in one, the only person to do so voluntarily. But my life had been so strange recently that this experience seemed almost normal.

As we travelled, I quizzed Besil about how Carnacans chose a route. The vehicle could be used either as a car with wheels or in hover mode so, theoretically, it could follow a very direct route. Besil explained that any route was a compromise. Certainly, when travelling over somewhere like the Bog of Allen, it made sense to use a route avoiding roads so as to minimise interaction with human traffic. But where the terrain was farmland with small fields and high hedges, it was preferable to follow human roads. In some cases, it made sense to travel just offshore. With our journey, the offshore option was of no real benefit because the Dublin/Wicklow Mountains meant that we would need to come back ashore north of Dublin. And since the Cooley Mountains meant we would either have to detour up Carlingford Lough or go offshore near Dundalk, we would be better staying ashore.

For much of the journey, we travelled on motorway. It felt strange to sit around forty-five miles per hour when all of the human traffic was moving much faster. Better this inconvenience than the risk of being detected and imperilling the entire humanity project was Besil's observation. As we progressed, she was curious about the bilingual road signs and street names. "Why two languages" she asked, "when only one is in common usage?" Many miles passed as I recounted the history of Ireland since the time of Henry II. Various English monarchs had sought to annex Ireland to their kingdom. Understandably, the native Irish resisted these attempts but, bit by bit, the English colonised most of the island. One of the more brutal campaigns was conducted by Oliver Cromwell, who exiled those who resisted to the poor lands in Connaught. Allied to the military campaigns were the plantations whereby English and Scottish people were either given land, which had been confiscated from the native Irish or sold that land at knockdown prices.

In the first half of the eighteenth century, a sustained attempt was made to suppress not just the Gaelic language, but also the Catholic faith professed by the great majority of the native population. These penal laws were draconian in the extreme. Curiously, the suppression of the use of Gaelic was much more effective than the attempted suppression of the Catholic faith. Possibly, part of the reason for this was the concept of martyrdom whereby dying for one's faith resulted in reward in the afterlife. In any event, people went to extraordinary lengths to practise their faith with masses being celebrated in remote locations, known as Mass Rocks. By the time part of the island obtained independence from Britain in 1922, the use of Gaelic as the vernacular tongue was restricted to a few small areas, mostly in the west of the island, known as Gaeltacht areas. I pointed out that the Cooley area, just a few miles from Knocknashee, was one such area. In my childhood, I had attended a Gaelic summer school in Omeath and recalled meeting the last surviving native speaker.

The Irish government took various steps to foster increased use of Gaelic. They introduced a requirement that any person employed by the government must be fluent in Gaelic. This regulation proved rather ineffective with many government employees having a very limited command of the language. This had brought about the comical situation where some who were stopped by the Gardai for traffic offences would seek to engage the Gardai in conversation in Gaelic. Many Gardai revealed their reluctance to have such a conversation by letting the offender off with a warning. Another measure was to declare that Gaelic was the official language of the state. Nevertheless, most business in the state parliament continued to be conducted in English. Bilingual signs followed on from the fiction that Gaelic was the country's official language.

Besil enquired if I knew Carlow or had ever been there before. I was able to tell her that a weekend in Carlow had been the cause of one of the turning points in my life. A romance that had developed over that weekend had led in due course to my separation from my wife after thirty-five years of marriage followed by divorce some four years later. The new relationship had given me some of the happiest days of my life but the old saying "blood is thicker than water" proved to be true. The relationship between her youngest son and me, after he moved back into her house after a marital breakdown, was best described as hostile. She invariably took his side irrespective of how obnoxious his behaviour was. I suspect that her actions were influenced by previous events when he had threatened suicide. It was a weird situation where a woman, who could be quite critical of the actions of any of her other three sons, seemed totally blind to how nasty the youngest of her offspring could be.

Clearly, Besil had viewed the recordings which I had viewed with Citas and Ixos because she asked if this had been the woman with me at Troy and Mostar. When I confirmed she was, Besil said that she was a very attractive woman.

The base near Carlow was remarkably similar to Knocknashee. We entered it in similar fashion, and the internal layout was pretty much identical. Malas was the senior person on the base, and he had assembled all the crew to greet their human visitor. Each seemed well versed in human customs because all came forward and shook my hand. He introduced one of them as the specialist linguist, Camas. The suggestion that Besil and I join Camas for a meal before starting work was most welcome.

My first impressions of Camas were not especially favourable. Compared with all of the crew at Knocknashee, he seemed to be of a lesser intellect. Certainly, his command of English was far inferior to that shown by Besil or even the others on her base. Even after making allowance for Besil's prolonged contact with me, he just lacked her ability. Once the meal and preliminary chitchat was over, we started down the same path as I had taken with Besil, and my first impression was confirmed. Things that Besil grasped after a single explanation required repeated explanations for Camas. The process should have been easier for him as he had the advantage of Besil's presence. She was able to reinforce my statements and explanations with a version in his own language. But still he struggled. So little progress did we make that, following the lesson, Besil suggested to me that we prolong our stay so that Camas had four face-to-face lessons instead of just one. This would entail spending an extra full day in Carlow, and I expressed my reluctance. She asked me to give the matter further thought during the couple of hours required to prepare the vehicle for the return journey.

During this time, I received news that was sufficiently startling to change my mind. I had not been paying much attention to the news in recent weeks. I had seen some stuff about a new virus in China but had been unaware of its arrival in Ireland and its rapid spread. Malas brought to my attention news coverage of a potential closedown of society, which seemed almost inevitable. I must have been one of a very, very few who actually welcomed the lockdown. Here was a solution to my problem. If bridge was cancelled, pubs closed and people only went out for essential reasons, my prolonged absence from Newry would not cause anywhere near as much difficulty. The only problem I could foresee was the possible arrival of correspondence requiring a prompt reply.

Even that problem was resolved when I discussed the matter with Besil. If I was prepared to take a chance and stay the extra day in Carlow, the Carnacans at Knocknashee would use the vehicle to ensure that I could collect my post from home at least once every four or five terrestrial weeks. Some visits could be made in the early hours of the morning to minimise the possibility of me being seen to appear out of thin air. As it happened, there was a vacant lot almost opposite my house where it would be possible for me to exit and re-enter the vehicle without any possibility of being observed even during daylight. Such an arrangement could not be implemented if she and I embarked on the trip to England she wished to undertake. That trip would require eight slow-time-speed days or seventeen terrestrial months. During that time, my post would have to wait. I suggested that I could leave a key to my house at the base and the post could be collected each night-time enabling it to be checked by me every nine weeks. Besil said that would not be possible. The was only one vehicle at the base, and she and I would be using it over in England. When I weighed everything, I concluded that the chance of urgent post arriving was vanishingly small. Was I really going to let a remote possibility prevent me from embarking on a remarkable quest. "No!" I decided. Thus began my first lengthy absence from Newry. It lasted almost two years until it was clear that the omicron wave had subsided. Even so, it was less than twelve full days at slow-time speed.

I was aware of the imposition of various travel restrictions, but Besil and I blithely ignored them. We spent eight of those days on a trip to Scotland, northern England, and part of the midlands visiting eight bases there. It was a weird sensation sitting just a couple of feet above the sea on the journey across the North Channel. If the sea had not been calm, Besil would not have attempted the crossing. During this trip, my faith in

Carnacan linguists was restored because five of them appeared to have similar ability to Besil, and the others were not far behind. I decided that Camas was the exception to the rule. Besil was aware of my lack of regard for Camas and made no attempt to persuade me differently. Instead, she explained that he was not a specialist linguist. The original choice for that base had taken ill the evening before the fleet departed Carnac. A replacement skilled linguist was not available, and Camas had volunteered for the task. Given the situation, his limited ability was better than nothing.

During the trip, I had dealings with many Carnacans. Whilst the primary purpose was to permit me face-to-face meetings with each linguist, others at each base were not going to waste an opportunity to talk to a human and seek answers on various topics. Many of their questions were easily answered, although frequently my answer would trigger further questions. However, some topics were beyond my competence. One of these was the nature of the COVID-19 virus, which was sweeping throughout world. Given Carnac's own experience of a deadly pandemic, they were understandably very interested in COVID. I was able to spend short periods outside the barrier during which I searched through websites and downloaded information and articles.

During one chat, I was advised that, from the evidence to hand, it did not look as if COVID would be as devastating as the virus had been on Carnac. Having said that, the original COVID virus had a mortality rate of around two per cent. Fortunately, the virus mutated into a less virulent version. What puzzled the Carnacans was the frequency with which pandemics had affected humanity. Experiencing the black death and Spanish flu just 250 years apart was unusual enough. To add in a second respiratory virus just a hundred years later was even more strange. I asked whether they thought it in any way likely that the virus had not come into being naturally. They reckoned that such a scenario could not be ruled out. The location of a laboratory experimenting on respiratory viruses in the region where the pandemic originated might or might not be coincidental. There simply was not enough evidence in the public domain on which to base a judgement due, in part at least, to a lack of transparency on the part of government in that country.

The responses of various governments did not impress the Carnacans. "Like headless chickens" was one scathing comment, which also revealed that my lessons on idiomatic English were bearing fruit. They were much more impressed with the speed with which effective vaccines and anti-viral drugs had been developed. Carnac might have been able to accomplish those tasks more quickly but not by a great deal. Humanity had certainly risen to the task.

Some incidents during that trip will remain in my memory for a long time. Besil and I had reached a base that was between Leeds and Barnsley. After a meal with some of the crew, we entered a room where we were to meet the linguist, Vasil. She was sitting with a white board about fifteen inches square in her hands. At first, I thought she was staring at it, but then I noticed that her eyes were almost closed. Besil whispered, "She seems to be meditating." After a few minutes, Besil suggested that I stand behind Vasil. When I did so, I saw a line drawing on the board of a piece of straw under which was written the legend: "I have drawn the short straw. Ha! Ha! Ha!" Vasil set down the board and said "Yes, I was the one who asked about the meaning of drawing the short straw." Even though both she and Besil maintained deadpan faces, I could not help but wonder whether the Carnacans had a sense of humour after all.

Besil and I passed the time during the long journeys between bases in conversation about a wide range of topics regarding both human and Carnacan activity. I suppose it was inevitable that she ask me whether I wished to learn her language and whether I thought I would be able to do so. "After all," she stated, "I have learned two of your languages." It was a challenge that I could not very well decline. Besil proved to be just as good a teacher as she was a pupil. Even so, my progress in learning Carnacan felt very slow. Some aspects of the language should have made it easier to learn. One was the most consistent spelling and pronunciation. Another was the absence of any regional dialects or idiomatic expressions. Conversely, other aspects rendered it more difficult to master. Carnacan did not have any prepositions, conjunctions or articles, either definite or indefinite. For example, "clanwe" meant "always strive," while "yashpak" meant "greater good." They certainly did not believe in any unnecessary wording.

Nor, it seemed, did they believe in any use of language which was not totally functional. When studying *War and Peace*, Besil had queried whether all of its content was historically accurate. I had said that I could not be certain, not realising that she was under the misapprehension that the book was a factual report of Napoleon's invasion of Russia. It was only when we started on *Animal Farm* and she said, "This cannot possibly be true," that I began to understand the situation. Fiction did not exist on Carnac. Nor did poetry. The only writing in existence was factual. Even after long hours spent discussing fiction, Besil still could not understand how one human could gain enjoyment from something invented in the mind of another.

This led me to ask what people on Carnac did to keep themselves entertained. They had no fiction to read, no films to watch and no music to listen to. Factor in an average of more than one hundred years in retirement. Surely, many must live in a state of chronic boredom. It emerged that just as emotions such as joy, anger, passion and amusement were not found on Carnac, neither were sadness nor boredom. Provided that they had contact with their fellow beings, Carnacans lived contentedly. Essentially, each individual regarded himself or herself not so much as an individual but as part of the community. I ventured the opinion that the thing on Earth closest to Carnac society was a colony of ants. Besil agreed that this was the case. All actions by ants were geared towards the greater good of the colony just as all actions by Carnacans sought to promote the greater good.

She acknowledged that there were many examples of groups of humans acting to further the common good, but these were outweighed by all those actions by individuals or small groups driven by self-interest. Besil said that it seemed that understanding self-interest was key to understanding humanity. I agreed, but, at the same time, I was keen to emphasise that it was accepted almost universally that acting in the common interest was preferable to selfish self-interest. By way of example, I cited the ten commandments that were fundamental to both Judaism and Christianity, with the latter religious belief of around one-quarter of humanity. Besil was unimpressed. "Ten commandments," she said, "and all except two are prohibitions. Positive action is preferable to abstinence from undesirable action." It was hard to disagree.

The subject having been broached, Besil wanted to know more about religious belief and practices. So, I outlined the creation story as propagated by Christianity, the New Testament account of redemption and the principal Christian beliefs. I also recounted the long history of schism and division and the less-than-exemplary conduct of popes, bishops, priests, and other religious entities. Besil asked whether I considered myself a Christian. I replied that I did not. Initially, she thought that my renunciation of Christianity was due to the evident corruption within the various churches, but I explained that this was not the case. My rejection was based on something much more fundamental.

I told her I would start at the very beginning. The Christian God is described as omnipotent, omniscient, infinitely good, and all loving. In the beginning, he existed on his own with a void where now exists the universe. His first act was to create heaven and the angels. But that was not a success because some of them, led by Lucifer, rebelled, and there was war in heaven. The white hats, led by Michael, prevailed, and Lucifer and his followers were cast into the eternal punishments of hell, which must have been created following the outbreak of the civil war. Next, God created the Garden of Eden and populated it with the first human couple, Adam and Eve. But Lucifer, now renamed Satan, corrupted Adam and Eve and caused them to commit sin, in other words an evil act. God decided to punish not just

Adam and Eve but also every one of the many hundreds of generations of their descendants.

Let us leave aside the manifest unfairness of punishing the unborn generations. Consider instead this question. How and why did evil come into being? Lucifer/Satan is seen as the epitome of evil and portrayed as devoted to seeking the downfall of any humans he can entice into evil. He is seen as the enemy of God. But who created Lucifer? The answer is God! Did this omniscient being not know that this first act of creation had brought into existence evil beings? Was this omnipotent being unable to correct this initial mistake? If there existed just God and a void, then evil did not exist. Evil came into being only once God started creating things. The inescapable conclusion is that this infinitely good being created evil. An equally inescapable conclusion is that the foundations on which Christianity is built are arrant nonsense.

Whilst I was not as au fait with the beliefs of other religions, what I did know gave me no reason to think that they were any less ridiculous than Christianity. Besil informed me that such religious belief did not exist on Carnac and, so far as she was aware, never had. She expressed amazement that the great majority of humanity appeared to have some sort of religious belief. In her view, this belief was a major contributor to an abdication of personal responsibility. She had listened to many recordings that included such religious expressions as "Deo volente", "God willing" or "Ins Allah." Did humans really believe that there was some kind of a puppet master controlling their destiny. I could not resist using the expression: "You are preaching to the converted." Following her quizzical expression, I had to explain the expression. Neither sarcasm nor irony had infiltrated Carnac yet.

Besil persisted in asking why, throughout almost 2,000 years, billions of people followed the god I had described. She could see some logic in following a god who had not failed in his creative attempts but not one who, having created evil, either could not or would not rid the world of it. Additionally, although humanity was unaware of Carnac, could there be any coherent explanation as to why this god created one planet where evil flourished and another where it did not?

My answer was that very few people thought about the creation story in any great depth. Even the most fervent Christians accepted that the description of God creating the world in six days and resting on the seventh could not be regarded as in any way historically accurate. The account had been written thousands of years ago long before the origins of modern science. Indeed, the story had previously been passed from one generation to the next in oral form. So, there existed this vague belief that although the details recorded in the Old Testament might be wrong, God had created the world.

The origins of Christianity can be found in Judaism. Jews regarded themselves as God's chosen people, a belief which seems very much at odds with the history of their travails as recorded in various books of the Old Testament. Exile in Babylon, slavery in Egypt, forty years wandering in the wilderness and even when they reached the promised land they were occupied and subjugated by the Romans. From the middle-ages onwards, they suffered all kinds of discrimination throughout Europe, culminating in the holocaust. Even during the good times, their behaviour did not set them aside as being in any way special. Their kings were men of the time who had large harems of concubines. There are stories of daughters having sex with a drunken father without any hint of criticism of such behaviour. Their god is sometimes depicted as given to asking his people to perform the most outrageous of acts to demonstrate their loyalty. Asking a father to sacrifice his son as an act of worship to a god is not the action of an all-loving and infinitely good god.

According to the New Testament, this god of the Jews who, unknown to them, had a tripartite nature, impregnated a virgin whilst leaving her a virgin. Her son was put to death by the Romans at the behest of Jewish religious authorities. Christians claim that this was the father sacrificing his son to secure salvation for humanity and to enable humans to avoid eternal punishment at his own hands. They also claim that the son rose from the dead after three days, was seen sporadically during the next forty days, and then headed back up to heaven, departing without any need for a spaceship.

The promise of eternity in heaven, provided one worships this god and refrains from sinful actions, has led billions to follow this god. Adding to the attraction is the ability to obtain forgiveness for any sins by confessing them to a priest and expressing remorse. Just how fervently people practise their faith is very much open to doubt. I told Besil that during my youth, almost all Catholics attended mass each Sunday, but in recent years, attendance had fallen by around three-quarters. This brought that church more in line with the Protestant churches. There is also the question of just what various people actually believe. With many Irish Catholics, their beliefs include some elements of paganism. In some other matters, a widespread belief is very much at odds with Catholic doctrine. For example, when a young child had died, most people refer to them as a little angel. Yet, the church states quite clearly that humans and angels are two very different species. Indeed, in the New Testament, it is stated that God has never called any angel his son, unlike the case with humans.

We spent some time discussing the various conflicts in which religion had played a part. Besil expressed the view that even though war because two groups had a difference of opinion regarding God could not be justified, she would distinguish between war between adherents of two quite different faiths and a war between two factions of the same religion. Therefore, she could just about understand the crusades but could not understand the various religious conflicts in Europe, including William's campaign against James in Ireland. I deepened her bewilderment further by telling her that William's campaign had been supported financially by the pope.

During our trip around the bases in Scotland and northern England, the inadequacy of my preparations was revealed. I ran out of clean clothes. I could have washed clothes at any of the bases, but the lack of drying facilities would have meant transporting wet clothes, which was not an appealing prospect. So, I agreed to Besil's suggestion that I try wearing a Carnacan robe. I was unable to wear it as they do for the simple reason that none of those available had been designed for anyone whose height exceeded five foot six. I am six feet tall, which meant that my robe came to just below the knee rather than the normal ankle length. Even so, I was very pleasantly surprised. I had expected the metallic nature of the fabric to make it uncomfortable. Instead, it felt more akin to cashmere. It was stain-resistant and just needed a couple of passes of an ultraviolet source to keep it hygienic. Even after we returned to Knocknashee and I had access to my own wardrobe and laundry facilities, I only wore my human clothing when on trips back home. On the base, I went native.

Chapter 7

Once back at Knocknashee, my conversations with its crew continued. Repeatedly, they returned to the competitive streak, which seemed to underly the aggression displayed by humans. "Why is it," asked Magas, "that humans feel the need to prove that they are better or can do something better than the next person?"

I said that I simply did not know. One theory, first developed by Charles Darwin, postulated that species evolved over time. Reproduction was not a perfect process and mutations could occur. The more successful mutations were those that conferred some advantage. The theory was commonly known as "the survival of the fittest" and suggested that competition was at the heart of human existence.

Certainly, competitiveness appeared to be innate rather than acquired through either education or societal pressure. Even young children vied with each other to show that they could run faster, jump higher or throw farther. I related how, when at primary school, we used an outdoor urinal. The wall behind the trough was rendered with sand cement. Regularly, we held competitions to see who could send a stream of urine furthest up the wall. I do not know whether our teachers were aware of this activity before one of our number really demonstrated his prowess by clearing the eight-foot-high wall. Unfortunately, wee Brother Collins was in the wrong place at the wrong time and was soaked. None of us were willing to identify the culprit so the entire class suffered punishment. Magas agreed that this story showed that any human activity could be the source of competition.

We examined how organised competition had existed for many centuries. Frequently, there was a military benefit to be had. The Romans held chariot races and gladiatorial contests. In medieval times, both jousting and archery competitions were held in England and elsewhere. Curiously, the original version of the Olympic Games, held in ancient Greece, involved a truce between the regions that participated. Certain other sports not involving combat also offered an indirect military benefit. These included horse-racing.

Organised competition in sports, which did not have a military connection, did not really get underway until the latter half of the nineteenth century. In football and cricket, leagues and championships were set up. In due course, international competitions were developed in football, involving both clubs and national teams. Arguably, the most significant development was the institution of the Olympic Games based on the previous Greek version. The founder, Baron de Coubertin, introduced a rather curious philosophy, which stressed that participation was more important than winning. He also restricted the games to amateurs. Initially, the banning of professionals was not that difficult, although it resulted in something of an imbalance in those competing. Those with inherited wealth or those belonging to a well-paid profession could more easily take time out not just to attend the games but to also train beforehand. Those who worked long hours just to survive did not find things so easy.

As time passed, the games became further and further removed from the original concept of friendly competition. Politics often intruded. The Nazi reaction to Jesse Owens, a black American athlete, winning one of the flagship events was far from friendly. Later years saw boycotts of games by the US and USSR and their respective allies.

Perhaps one of the most pernicious changes was the permitting of the participation of professionals. Over time, this morphed from allowing athletes to take part, who earned money from competing in events out-with the Olympics, to governments paying them large sums of money to spare them the necessity of holding down a job. In theory, this meant that the most talented would have the financial support needed to enable them to compete on behalf of their country. In practice, things were not quite so straightforward. The best talent would, almost inevitably, win significant prize money. Should their state funding be withdrawn and reallocated to lesser talent? As it happened, the budget for financial support to competitors in any sport was linked to the number of medals won.

The advent of big money being bankrolled into athletics, as with any sport, increased the temptation to cheat. The principal method of cheating was the use of performance-enhancing drugs. One cannot know the extent to which this occurred before drug testing became commonplace even out of competition. But prior to professionalism, the glory from winning an Olympic medal or a world championship would have been scant compensation for the potential health risks. Increasing prize money and government funding altered the equation. Now, athletics could provide a very wealthy lifestyle.

In some countries, the situation was even worse. Instead of cooperating with the sports' governing bodies and the anti-doping agencies, these governments, thankfully few in number, actually organised and ran a doping programme for their athletes. Various stratagems were employed, including tampering with blood- and urine-testing procedures. On a temporary basis, these doping programmes were extremely effective. Some of the world records set by athletes who participated in them stood for many years.

Whatever the difficulties experienced by athletics and other sports involving individual performance, the situation in one team sport was much, much worse. Football. This time, the use of performance-enhancing drugs was not the problem. Indeed, the problem lay not with any of the participants but with the spectators. Magas was puzzled when I first told him this. "Surely, spectators play no part in the game," he said. His bewilderment increased as I described the behavioural problems associated with football supporters especially during the sixties, seventies, and eighties. Back in those early days of professional football, almost all of the team were from the area in which the football ground was situated. Similarly, all of the supporters were also from that area. Then the transfer market became more and more important, and teams used a greater number of players bought from other teams. Strangely, the increasing use of players who were not from the club's natural hinterland did nothing to diminish the fervour of the supporters. These supporters watched football as if the result was a matter of life and death. Indeed, one club manager famously quipped: "Football is not a matter of life and death. It is much more important than that!"

The fervour of the supporters was, to an extent, understandable if one regarded each set of supporters as a tribe from a local area. The team they supported was competing on behalf of that area even if it did use other players who could be viewed as hired guns. This fervour sometimes led to violence between two sets of supporters.

Such violence was never excusable. But the advent of television helped bring about a situation where the violence was not just inexcusable but inexplicable. Television coverage of football matches led to many people becoming supporters of teams based in areas far away from where they lived. At the same time, better transport connections meant that it was possible for such supporters to travel long distances to watch their team play. These supporters had no connection whatsoever to the area in which their team was based. Their support was often for as flimsy a reason as that they liked the name, it was the first team they saw win on television, or one of the players shared their surname. Yet, they frequently were guilty of the same violent conduct as those who supported their local club.

The violent conduct was not confined to the football ground. Often, fighting occurred well away from the ground both before and after the match. I told Magas that when I attended university in Manchester in the early seventies, the city centre at teatime on a Saturday was a dangerous place to be, especially on the two Saturdays when City and Utd met.

Increasingly, I found the conversations about competitiveness and aggression with Magas and others less and less enjoyable. It always came as a pleasant relief to talk to Besil about linguistic matters. It certainly helped that she was strikingly beautiful to go along with her great intellect and linguistic ability. I ceased to be surprised at her growing command of idiomatic English. So, it came as a complete bombshell when, as restrictions were relaxed as omicron subsided, she asked me out!

Actually, what happened was that she expressed a wish to see whether she could pass herself off as a human if she was in the company of humans other than me. Initially, I dismissed the idea as far too risky but the more I thought about it the more feasible it seemed. After all, her command of English was better than many inhabitants of Newry, and her accent, though far removed from typical Norn Iron, was fairly neutral. If anything, it had a faint Eastern European tinge so she could be introduced as somebody originally from somewhere, like Slovenia, who had spent quite a bit of time in London.

One obvious difficulty was that she could not appear in her normal garb. So, I then found myself traipsing around Marks and Spencer, Next, and other shops purchasing female clothing and shoes. As a precaution, I did the shopping in Belfast where there was little chance of the shop assistant knowing me and asking any awkward questions. Besil had been quite relaxed about me measuring her vital statistics. I calculated she was either a size six or size eight, so I bought both sizes in each of four outfits so as to give her a choice of what she wanted to wear. With the underwear, I compromised between extremely sexy and utilitarian thinking that a little femininity would not go amiss. Shoes were more problematic as I did not like the idea of her being unable to try them on before wearing them. Luckily, I was able to buy an old Clarks shoe gauge from a charity shop. She was a size three, which would restrict the choice available. However, I was able to purchase several pairs of both flat shoes and others with a two-inch heel.

As far as I could tell, Besil was pleased with my choices of outfits, but she would not tell me which she would wear on our night out. We agreed with Ixos that it should take place before the UK moved on to British Summer Time in late March. It was essential that Besil did not leave the vehicle before darkness fell and, during BST, that would leave very little time for us to walk to the Phoenix and enjoy some conversation with my friends. So, we parked in the vacant lot opposite my house around 7.30 p.m. on Wednesday, 16 March 2022. Besil looked quite stunning in her chosen outfit and had surprised me by opting for high heels. Apparently, she had spent quite some time practising walking in them, having never previously worn anything like them.

On our walk from Canal Street to the pub, we met Peter O'Hare, who was heading homewards after having taken his dog out for its evening walk. As we chatted for a few minutes, the dog rubbed up against me looking for me to pet it. But when Besil attempted to pet it, the dog's reaction was very different. It backed away and growled. Peter was most apologetic, saying that he could not understand it. The dog was very even-tempered, and he had never seen it behave in that manner. I have often wondered whether the dog was able to do something no human ever managed which was to recognise Besil as being extra-terrestrial.

Our arrival in the Phoenix caused quite a stir. Some of my friends made a point in coming over, expressing pleasure at seeing me again after such a long interval. Naturally, there was a bit of banter with a couple of them asking me to introduce them to my granddaughter. I fed them the agreed cover story that she was the daughter of a second cousin who had settled in Slovenia. She had spent several years in London. Now she was involved in trying to discover more about her family tree. John, one of my friends, asked her if I had bored her with an account of how I was a direct descendant of Robert the Bruce.

We had agreed in advance that it might be ill-advised for Besil to drink sufficiently to render her intoxicated. She had no prior experience with alcoholic drink, and, in any event, she was the designated driver. A white wine spritzer looked to be a good choice. If necessary, after the first, she could unobtrusively stick to white lemonade. She drank two small bottles of sauvignon blanc, diluted with white lemonade, without any noticeable effect.

The evening went remarkably well with everybody buying the cover story. From her contributions to the conversation, nobody could have suspected that Besil was anything other than what she purported to be. I noted with humour her occasional use of idiomatic expressions especially when she referred to my youngest brother as "that gaunch." After a while, one of the assembled company started singing along to the background music. Somehow this led to Besil being asked if she could sing. Before I could intervene, she said that she could and asked Darren the bar manager to turn off the music. She then absolutely wowed us with a truly wonderful, note-perfect rendition of *The Fields of Athenry*. Her voice would not have been out of place in grand opera. I could scarcely believe my ears. The others were not going to let her off with just the one song. They demanded more. She obliged. *The Rose* was followed by *Only the Rivers Run Free*. Then came *Don't Cry for Me, Argentina, Grace, Danny Boy, Raglan Road*, and others. One of my friends suggested that she could be only a very distant relation of mine because I am a genuine crow. Who knows how long the session would have lasted if Darren had not intervened around 12.30 a.m., stating that however much he was enjoying the singing, he needed to get home to his bed in Rathfriland. At this, somebody asked if she would finish the session with *The Soldiers' Song*. She did and attracted even more adulation by singing the Gaelic version of *Amhrain na Bhfeinn*. I was blown away.

As we were leaving, Darren told us that he was hoping to reinstate live music on Sunday afternoons and evenings. He would be delighted to book Besil for one or more sessions. After tonight, word would spread about this phenomenal singer, and he was confident that for any session featuring her, the Phoenix would be bunged. Besil thanked him for the offer but said that she would not be in Newry for the next few months. Hopefully, she would be back by October or November when she would be delighted to take Darren up on his offer. We agreed that I would keep Darren posted on her plans.

We left the Phoenix, accompanied by Damien, whose house was, thankfully, reached before we reached the vehicle. He was keen to prolong the night and pressed us to come in for a nightcap. We declined, citing an early flight later that day.

When we were safely ensconced in the vehicle, Besil turned to me and said, "Well? Say something." I scarcely knew where to start. That her interaction with a group of people she had never met before had been indistinguishable from that of a human. Her knowledge of the lyrics of many songs. Her amazing vocal performance. Each on its own was impressive, but together, they were utterly remarkable. Besil reminded me that, for years, she had studied recordings of interactions between humans, so it was relatively easy to mimic such behaviour. Besides, she had benefitted from my personal tuition that had enabled her to become familiar with idiomatic usage. Learning the song lyrics had not been difficult. After all, had I not brought a CD player and various CDs to the base. I said that I was still impressed at her mastery of the lyrics. However, I felt it necessary to offer some advice on her choice of songs. Her selections may have gone down well in the Phoenix but would not have been appreciated in other venues. Similarly, there were many songs which the patrons in the Phoenix would not want to hear. Perhaps she should get me to vet her song list if there were going to be any future performances. What I really wanted to know was how she had learnt to sing and, not just to sing, but to sing as perfectly as had ever been achieved by any human. And how had she kept it secret from me? She said that Ixos had helped her to a great extent. They had used computers to analyse the musical harmonics. She then tried to reproduce those harmonics using her vocal cords whilst Ixos recorded her efforts. Next, they overlaid the original recording with Besil's effort to identify any defects. Soon, not only was Besil matching the original but surpassing it. Their computer programme was able to identify instances of the human singer failing to produce the required note perfectly, and Besil was able to surpass the original performance. A trained opera singer might have been able to understand her explanation of how she could modify the sounds produced by her vocal cords, but it was quite beyond me. Given that music and song were unknown on Carnac, and that she was the first Carnacan to attempt to sing, her performance verged on the miraculous.

Ixos greeted us when we entered the base. "It must have been a good night to keep you out so late," he said. I described the evening's events, taking care to acknowledge the part played by Ixos in Besil's preparation. "I just operated the machinery," he said. She did all the difficult work." Besil was rather self-deprecating. I suspected she did not fully realise just what she had achieved. It was only when I got Citas to bring up some recordings of ordinary people singing in the street and had Ixos overlay them on a professional recording of the songs that it dawned on her just how good she was. She was on a par at least with the best humanity could offer. Ixos seemed to focus just as much on how she had interacted with different people without attracting any suspicion. The reason for this soon became apparent.

Ixos believed that they had reached the stage when they could progress from remote observation to interaction with humans. The problems caused by solar radiation meant that this interaction must be confined to half of the terrestrial year. Besil had been the obvious choice to be the first to venture into human society. She had the best command of English and had spent more time with me than any of the others. Her visit to the Phoenix would have been considered a success even without her singing success. This led Ixos to conclude that he and some of the others could also interact with humans. Citas, Magas, and Napel were three of the crew who should be able to pull it off. All they needed was some assistance from me.

The most obvious help required was sourcing human clothing. Ixos listened as I explained how the size difference between the two peoples acted to restrict the choice of available clothing, whether male or female. The sizes they needed were at the extreme lower end of the range available, dipping down into children's sizes in some instances. At one point, Ixos expressed gratitude at my willingness to purchase the necessary garments. "Your expenditure on books and clothing is mounting up," he said. "We don't want to drain your resources." I was happy to explain that my prolonged stay in slow-time speed had served to increase my bank balance by over £30,000 whilst the books cost less than £1,000 and the clothing would cost less than £2,000. He need not worry about my finances.

I pointed out that what was needed was a range of venues to be visited by the crew. It would not be sensible for all of them to accompany me, even one at a time to the Phoenix. One person of small stature would not attract any attention but a succession of small people, especially male, might provoke suspicion. I suggested we use a couple of different pubs, a couple of restaurants, one of my bridge clubs, and whist night at the Shamrocks. Needless to say, I had to explain both bridge and whist. Mastering either of these should be much easier than learning to sing. Given that British Summer Time was about to begin, these visits would need to wait until October. Ixos agreed.

As it was, taking a Carnacan to bridge by October was a tough ask, timewise. Having taught bridge to beginners both in Newcastle and Dunleer, I knew that most people required around fifteen two-hour lessons before one would contemplate taking them into a bridge club. There are exceptions. I was one such exception. But I had less than four full days to bring somebody with no previous experience of card games up to an acceptable standard. I need not have worried. Having brought my set of boards and bidding boxes to the base, I set about teaching a group of four. The first task was to teach them whist, which can be regarded as a precursor of bridge. An hour was sufficient to bring them all to a standard comparable to the better players in the Shamrocks. I decided that Citas would be the one to attend the Shamrocks. All four of them displayed a real aptitude for bridge. It was a close call between Ixos and Besil as to who was better. I decided to take Ixos to bridge. Recalling my own experience with thought-reading, I detailed the relevant provisions in the Laws of Bridge. Ixos assured me that not only would he not read my thoughts, but he would not read our opponent's thoughts either.

Besil had provided to Carnac a comprehensive report of her visit to the Phoenix. Carnac congratulated her on making the first Carnacan visit inside a human building. They looked forward to

receiving reports of the other proposed visit. They also requested that I or some of the crew place recording devices inside some
buildings. The bulk of that task fell to me. The Cathedral, library,
bus station, Tesco, M & S, Sainsbury, Lidl, and other shops were
obvious locations. Next came the Phoenix, Joseph Magee's, and
the Bridge Bar. I also managed to install one in Goldilocks, the
hairdressing salon I attended. It was one of the trickiest, but I
got lucky. A customer brought with her a six-week-old baby, and
I placed the device whilst Janet and Sarah were busy cooing over
the pram. Besil and the other females in the crew seemed fascinated by the various procedures and treatments they witnessed.

Another matter with which Ixos asked me to assist was an
investigation into how well, or otherwise, Carnacans could tolerate alcoholic drinks. Besil had coped well in the Phoenix, but
others might not. So, I was tasked with bringing a selection of
drinks to the base. This necessitated the same taxi journey as
when I brought the books, although, on this occasion, I needed
three trips from my friend's house. I hoped that three days were
sufficient for the investigation. Preliminary results showed that
Carnacans reacted to alcohol in similar fashion to humans but
that their tolerance was around fifty per cent greater.

Organising clothing could be approached in a more leisure-
ly fashion. Again, I used shops in Belfast to purchase a mix-
ture of casual and more formal male clothing. Another matter
to be sorted was the question of surnames for the Carnacans.
Surnames were not used on their planet. Instead, they had a
system of nomenclature similar, in some ways, to that used in
Gaeltacht areas. In the Gaeltacht, a man was known by his own
first name, followed by his father's and his grandfather's. An example would be Paddy, Micky, Hughie. On Carnac, a man used
his own first name, followed by his mother's, then his father's.
For a woman, it was her name, then her father's, then her mother's. I explained that whilst a visit to the pub or a restaurant
would not need a surname to be used, bridge and whist would.
I suggested a few possibilities. The most obvious was one that
referenced their home plant. And so came about Ixos Carney.

Given the location of the base, that old film Darby O'Gill and the Little People suggested another. Magas was not keen on O'Gill but thought that Magas Magill sounded well. For Besil, I offered a choice of Nightingale or Linnet, much to the puzzlement of the Carnacans. Once they had the reference to singing birds explained to them, Besil opted for Linnet. Citas Cook also came about reflecting his status as navigator. Jamil chose the alliterative Juniper.

By good fortune, my regular bridge partner in Warrenpoint was on a foreign holiday in early November, so the second of that month saw Ixos and I parking the vehicle on the golf course close to the clubhouse. I introduced Ixos as somebody I had come to know during the period when I had played regularly in the Bankers Bridge Club in Dublin. He and I had first played together on one of the nights when there was a draw for partners. We had got on well together and had since played together a few times in competitions down south. With the Bankers being one of the strongest clubs in the country, there was a general expectation amongst the Warrenpoint members that he would be a very good player. They were not disappointed. I played well that night, but Ixos was even better. Any player bringing off three squeezes and a scissors coup in the one session would be well pleased. For anyone to do it after just a handful of lessons was almost unbelievable. In its own way, it was just as remarkable as Besil's singing. Our score of 77.8% was the highest ever recorded in the club. We received a bit of banter at the end of the session. "Does this mean Pat Lynchehaun will have to look for a new partner?" Pat was my regular partner with whom I had enjoyed good success within the club, but he was not in the same league as Ixos. Were Ixos and I to play in the Camrose trials by which the Northern Ireland team was selected, I would have every confidence that we could finish in the top three. I informed the questioner that I would not be dropping Pat and that Ixos would likely be an infrequent visitor. Ixos added that he would be very happy to play with a different partner on some future occasion prompting several members to give him a note of their mobile number.

Two nights later, Citas and I headed to the Shamrocks. In the absence of a safe parking spot any closer to the venue, we left the vehicle opposite my house and taxied it there to escape the heavy showers that were about. Citas seemed a little apprehensive about playing with a succession of strange partners. I told him he had nothing to worry about, that he was a better player than most of them. The advice I gave him was not to criticise any play by his partner irrespective of how stupid it might have been. Similarly, he should accept without demur any criticism levelled at him no matter how baseless it might be. I was only at the same table as Citas twice but, from halfway through the evening, I listened to people singing his praises telling me how good a player my friend was. It came as no surprise when his scorecard revealed he had accumulated 162 tricks in the twenty hands, winning by a margin of seven tricks. Paddy usually offered me a lift home and was happy to take Citas, as well. Once we were back in the vehicle, Citas was quick to offer his prize money to me saying that not only had I paid his entry fee but had spent a lot on his clothing. I refused it, telling him he might find it useful if he ever visited the Phoenix or some other pub. I was already thinking that, sooner or later, Ixos would suggest that two Carnacans visited Newry without me.

Friday of the following week provided a most enjoyable experience. I took Jamil to the Oliver, a restaurant which always had an interesting menu, and the food was always excellent. A couple of acquaintances of mine were in the restaurant and their envious glances were very gratifying. Jamil behaved as if this was something with which she was very familiar. Her choice of food was the same as mine. I got her to order first with no knowledge of my choices, and she went for scallops as starter followed by turbot. So, did I. She quizzed me on my life history and then surprised me. She said that it seemed that when a man took a woman out for dinner, they often finished up having sex together. I told her I would be delighted to shave sex with her again but that she must not feel obliged to do so. She said that she wanted to do it because she wanted to give me pleasure. I was very happy to go along with her suggestion. We enjoyed an excellent meal and strolled back to the vehicle.

The following day, Besil made a request. She wanted to go shopping. She realised that most shops were essentially open only during daylight hours. The best option was Tesco, which, even though it had not returned to twenty-four-hour opening, stayed open until eleven o'clock. Visiting the supermarket would advance her understanding of an essential part of human existence. I was happy to accede to her request, and she and I parked the vehicle in the usual spot and walked around to Tesco. To make the visit as authentic as possible, Besil had sole control over what we purchased. Additionally, I gave her my club card, debit card, and PIN, with guidance on how to use both. I also thought it was an opportune time to use some club-card vouchers, which were about to expire. It was the longest visit I have ever made to the supermarket. Besil was curious as to the use made of many of the items on display. She was fascinated by the various cosmetics on display. Unsurprisingly, lipstick, face powder, deodorant, and perfume found their way into the shopping trolley. The clothing on display did not impress her, and she said it was obvious that I had not purchased her clothing in this shop.

The warning that the shop was going to close in fifteen minutes had sounded by the time we reached the checkout. It was as well there were two of us as neither would have been able to carry the stuff unaided. I helped to place our purchases on the conveyor but otherwise left Besil to deal with proceedings. One would have thought she had been doing it all her life. The banter between her and the checkout assistant was mostly at my expense. One remark was, "I only brought him with me because you need a donkey to carry a heavy load." If it had been a human making such a comment, I might have taken umbrage, but instead I viewed it as further evidence of Besil's remarkable progress. Walking back to the vehicle, she asked me how she had done. "Hee-haw," I replied and thought I saw the faintest of grins. Perhaps she was acquiring the beginnings of a sense of humour.

The weeks flew past, and, in due course, the advent of British Summer Time curtailed the Carnacan visits to Newry. Besil suggested that we undertake another trip to the bases in England. The remote lessons involving the northern bases had continued with most of the linguists making excellent progress. These linguists were now seeking additional written material. The linguists in the southern bases were all seeking to join the programme. The volume and weight of the books and other items needed for both sets of bases would be too much for a single vehicle so the linguist from Carlow was roped in. He travelled to Knocknashee and took on board the additional books for the northern bases. Besil and I would take the stuff for the southern bases as she wanted me to visit each of them.

Ixos was aware that the trip to England meant that I would be away from Knocknashee for around eighteen terrestrial months. Thus, I would miss the whole of the next bridge season. Rather than miss out, he asked Camas to travel around the northern bases as quickly as possible so that he could be back at Knocknashee by October or November. He also wished Camas to stay at the base until Besil and I returned. This would make the vehicle from Carlow available for trips into Newry. Camas readily agreed, unsurprisingly, because Ixos indicated that he would be included in the trips into Newry.

I was a little taken aback when Besil said she hoped I was bringing with me some human clothing. When I asked why, she said that she was hoping we would get the chance to visit some towns and cities in England. She also thought that others on the bases we would be visiting would also wish to have such an opportunity. She added that it might be an idea to bring my debit card and some cash. Ixos confirmed that some of the other bases had already indicated to him that some of their crew wished to meet not just me but other humans. He and Besil had already stowed some of the clothing, both male and female, that I had supplied. Doubtless, I would be able to acquire more once over there.

Ixos also said that he had received communications from both Carnac and various bases in the US. So much progress had been

made in Ireland and the northern British bases that they wanted me to consider a prolonged trip to the bases in the US and
Canada. I did not need to decide now, but I could think about it
during this trip. He added that the Atlantic crossing could not
be made in the base vehicle. They would need a spaceship to
collect Besil and me from Knocknashee and drop us off at an
American base. The spaceship would also carry the base vehicle
from Antarctica, which was seldom used. This would facilitate
visits to American towns and cities by Besil, other Carnacans
and me. On hearing this, I was keen to hear whether the spaceship would enter space or just fly like a human aeroplane. I was
disappointed when told it would be like a conventional flight.

The proposed trip to the American bases sounded as though
it would be much lengthier than the trips to mainland Briton.
With over fifty bases and great distances to be travelled, it would
take a minimum of ten terrestrial years. From what Besil was
saying, she expected us to be visiting American towns and cities, which could make the trip much longer. Since I am unfamiliar with all of those places, it was likely that the first outing in any locality would be a reconnaissance to be followed by
another outing when both our borrowed vehicle and the local
base vehicle would be used. On the assumption that the trip
would last twenty years or so, undertaking it would effectively
sever all links with my friends, almost all of whom would likely
be deceased by the time I returned. I was reminded of the cus-
tom that developed during the mass emigration from Ireland
in the aftermath of the famine. Because those emigrating to
America were most unlikely to ever return, what was known as
an American wake was held prior to their departure.

But as Besil, Ixos and I continued our discussion, it became
clear that this second trip to mainland Britain would last much
longer than the previous trip. Similar considerations applied
to visits to English or Welsh towns and cities as did to their
American counterparts. I was not totally unfamiliar with many
of the places involved but had not been to some of them for
several years. Passage of time was in itself sufficient to make a

reacquaintance reconnaissance desirable, and if one factored in the devastation caused to the hospitality industry by COVID, such reconnaissance became essential. That being the case, I could be away for four or five years.

That realisation prompted me to put into place certain arrangements. I knew that my debit and credit cards would require replacement within the next couple of years. What I did not know was whether either the Civil Service Pension Scheme or the National Insurance Pension Scheme were likely to write to me seeking confirmation I was still alive. There was also the matter of my medication for hypertension and low thyroid function. I was reassured when Ixos said the last matter would not be a problem because any of the bases could provide me with equivalent medication. To counter the other problems, I provided Ixos with a key to my house so that he could collect my mail on a regular basis. Anything in the nature of a debit or credit card would be brought to wherever I was by Camas. Letters could be read to me and, as I was taking my laptop and printer with me, I could deal with them just as easily as if I were at home. Obviously, other arrangements would be needed if I went on the American trip.

The trip took much longer than I had anticipated. Yes, we completed our tour of the southern bases in just under five years. But, during that period, we had been bombarded by messages from the northern bases. Having heard what was happening farther south, they did not want to miss out. So, we revisited each northern base and guided them through their first steps in interaction with humans other than me.

Some bases were more fortunate than others. Those that were visited during the summer period when daylight hours were longer were restricted in the choice of venue. When daylight was only fading at half past ten, the options were supermarkets that stayed open through the night or nightclubs. Indeed, with a couple of bases in the northern part of Scotland, the hours of darkness during the height of summer were so short that going there in June or July would have been pointless. This meant that we could not follow the optimal route, resulting in a greater distance being travelled.

Most of our visits followed a similar pattern. On reaching the vicinity of the base, Besil and I would undertake a preliminary reconnaissance in daylight hours without leaving the vehicle. This guided our later reconnaissance once darkness had fallen when we identified one or more parking places and checked out pubs, clubs or restaurants. We were then able to act as guides for others from the base for one or more visits. Having just our vehicle and the local base vehicle at our disposal restricted the number on any visit to a maximum of four. Given that they are a very unemotional race, lacking in passion, the Carnacans displayed excellent interpersonal skills. And it was gratifying to note that those from the northern bases, who had the benefit of my programme in written English, all had an excellent command of idiomatic English. I knew that, in the past, I had been successful as a bridge teacher and, fifty years previously, when teaching first aid. Now I could see the fruits of my labours as an English teacher, and it felt good.

Although the idea of visits by Carnacans to local towns and cities had been their own, I felt a certain responsibility lay with me. If I had not stumbled across Knocknashee, none of this would be happening. So, I left £2,000 in cash at each base. I could afford it, and it would not have been right to give them a taste of interaction with humanity without leaving them the wherewithal to continue that interaction.

Around one-third of the way through our trip, I started to wonder how Besil felt about spending so much time at normal time speed. She said that it was not a problem. After all, she would experience the same length of life irrespective of the time speed in which she lived. So, there was no downside. She was very conscious of her privileged position. Those from the other bases were limited to interacting with humans in just the one area. On average, each could participate in only one-tenth of the trips to the local town or city. Even such a restricted number of interactions with local humans was something that only a few hundred Carnacans had enjoyed. She was able to take part in many more trips in different areas, meaning she was uniquely privileged.

One task where she was keen to do more involved the purchase of female clothing. Most clothes shops were closed during the hours when she could leave the protection of the base or vehicle. She believed that she would be better at selecting clothes for the other females. So, I found myself wandering around the likes of Marks and Spencer, Next, and various boutiques photographing different outfits taking care to make a note of where each batch of photographs had been taken. Besil would then choose which outfits I should purchase. Many was the strange look I received from shop assistants. Fortunately, all of them bought the fiction that I was involved in the provision of costumes and props to a drama group.

I do not know what each Carnacan thought of the humans they met. The few from whom I received feedback expressed some surprise at how peaceable those they had met seemed to be. The one situation where this was never the case was the football stadium. The Carnacans were able to attend midweek matches during winter months. All who did so found the adrenalin-charged atmosphere disturbing. Invariably, there was at least verbal aggression between the two sets of supporters, and, on a couple of occasions, the Carnacans has witnessed physical violence outside the stadium. I could just imagine the comments from Magas.

During the trip, we received periodic updates from Ixos. Mostly, these described the various visits to Newry by the crew from the base. One report was straight out of left field. I had left a large amount of cash with Ixos with which he could fund meals in restaurants, drinks in pubs, and the like. This had been augmented by Citas, who came first in the whist at the Shamrocks four times in the space of five visits. But then Citas had a stroke of luck that caused an unforeseen problem. He had been persuaded to use some of his whist prize money to enter the Shamrocks lottery. On his next visit, he discovered he had won the jackpot, which stood at £8,300. The club had waited until they next saw him before making out the cheque because he had been entering the bridge using just Citas. I had to admire how well he had thought on his feet. He had asked them to make out the cheque to Anthony O'Gallagher, explaining that he did not have a bank account. He had been declared bankrupt and had just exited bankruptcy. Whilst I expressed admiration for Citas's quick thinking, and sent my congratulations on his good fortune, I advised Ixos that it was important that he got the cheque to me as soon as possible. Once I had explained that cheques were only valid for six months, Ixos said he would travel with Camas to bring it to me. I could then lodge it to my Ulster Bank account via a Nat West branch in England. Ixos thought that I should treat the money as recompense for my expenditure on behalf of Carnacans. I told him that the money properly belonged to Citas and reiterated that my personal wealth would have increased by more than £100,000 during the trip to England. What Citas did with the money was entirely up to him although I imagined he would use it to fund expenditures by all of the crew.

Whilst at a base just west of London, I could not resist the temptation to revisit an old haunt. Besil and I took a chance and parked the vehicle in Hyde Park. We could have walked straight to our destination, but Besil wished to experience the tube system. After a brief jaunt, we exited the Underground at Notting Hill Gate and strolled along Bayswater Road to a certain Italian restaurant. Luckily enough they were able to accommodate us. As we studied the menu, I noticed the waiter eyeing us with a quizzical look on his face. When he came over to take our order he said, "How is life at the *Guardian* these days?" He had remembered me even though my last visit to his restaurant had been some fifteen years previously. I recounted the story to Besil. My wife and I had enjoyed a meal there on a trip to London. Three weeks later, we were back in London and took my older sister there. When taking our order, the same waiter had said, "You were here a couple of weeks ago," to which I had replied, "Yes.

Did you read the report?" I then enquired as to whether he read the *Guardian* newspaper, which I thought most unlikely. Later, while I was in the gent's, he asked Mary and Maeve if I really was the restaurant critic from the *Guardian*. Over the following few years, we visited the restaurant whenever we were in London. When my youngest son was graduating from Imperial College, I asked him to book a table for all eight of us who would be spending the evening together. He had gone there one lunchtime and spoke to the chef who was the waiter's father. We had never spoken to the man, yet he told Kevin, "Yes. We know Mr O'Gallagher. He has been here before." When we reached the restaurant, my friend Tony was greatly impressed. He and I were walking in front of the others. About twenty yards from the restaurant, the waiter, who had been standing in the doorway, came towards us with outstretched hand. "Long time, no see!" he exclaimed. He was right. Over a year had elapsed since I had last been there.

On this occasion, I thought I would chance my arm. Even though the dish was not on the menu, I asked if it would be possible to have Tournedos Rossini as my main course and was delighted when he agreed. Besil said she would have the same. In answer to my enquiry, he informed me that his father had died around eighteen months previously having never totally recovered after contracting COVID.

The food was, as always, excellent. My enjoyment was enhanced even further when I settled the bill. The rather pricy bottle of Barolo was on the house!

The following day, Ixos and Camas arrived at the base. In addition to the cheque, Ixos brought a new debit card that had just been issued. "See?" he exclaimed. "We, Carnacans, can also multitask!" Even though he uttered the words in his customary deadpan manner, I could not help but wonder whether he was acquiring the first vestiges of a terrestrial sense of humour.

Ixos was also responsible for prolonging our stay near London. He wanted to experience that city. Newry might be nominally a city but, in reality, was just a medium-sized town. At his request,

we really cut loose. The highlight came when I managed to book
a table for six in Le Gavroche. The three vehicles at our disposal
were parked in Hyde Park, and Ixos, Camas, Besil, Merel, Pikel,
and I took the tube into the city centre. It was well I was now a
wealthy man because Gavroche does not do cheap. The bill came
to almost £2,000. Three bottles of wine costing £360 each certainly inflated it, nor was that the end of the extravagance. A
round of cocktails in a high-end nightclub set me back just over
£200. As the tube had finished for the night, by the time we left
the club, we taxied it back to Bayswater Road getting the drivers to drop us off at one of the hotels on the road.

Chapter 8

November 2029 had arrived by the time Besil and I arrived back at Knocknashee. Ixos had the decency to allow me a night's sleep before asking about what decision I had reached regarding the American trip. I told him I was happy to go but not just yet. I had three reasons for wanting to delay the trip. Two of them involved my own benefit whilst the third would benefit the Carnacans.

The first reason was very simple. Much as I enjoyed Carnacans' company, I still missed my human friends. Seven years had elapsed since I had last seen them, and I did not know which, if any, of them were still alive. One thing was certain. Once I embarked on the American trip, it was extremely unlikely I would ever see them again. If one estimated the duration of the trip at thirty terrestrial years, not only would my friends all be dead, but my children could well be also. My eldest son would be in his eightieth year. I was quite happy to commit to the Carnacan project but wanted some time with my fellow humans first.

The second reason was a bit quirky. I was in my fifties when I took up the game of bridge. Once I acquired a couple of decent partners, I enjoyed some success. The NIBU had a grading system involving the acquisition of masterpoints that were awarded to those who did best in various competitions. There were two types of masterpoint, local and red or national. Once one acquired one hundred red points, one was designated as expert. Before COVID hit and disrupted bridge competitions, I had been closing in on expert status. If I teamed up with one of the good players with whom I was on friendly terms, I believed I could achieve expert status within two years.

Thirdly, I wanted to be able to dispense cash to the American bases in similar amounts to that given to the English bases. I would be able to obtain some cash from automated teller machines but not in the quantities required. I explained to Ixos that the US used a different currency to the UK and that Canada used a different one yet again. Whereas I could go into a bank here or in England and withdraw large sums of cash, I could not do that in the US or Canada. I would need to obtain a large stash of US dollars before I went. This would take a little time as I did not want to request more than $2,000 at a time, and I wished to take around $100,000 with me. A delay of two years would also give me time to purchase a good stock of clothing and the three hundred books required.

I suggested departure should take place in fourteen slow-time-speed days' time, or roughly two and a half terrestrial years. Ixos replied that he would need to consult Carnac but that he did not foresee any disagreement. A short while later, he confirmed that Carnac had agreed to my proposal.

The time leading up to departure for America simply flew by. On calling in to the Phoenix, I was delighted to find Marty, John Boy, and Woodsy all hale and hearty. Even though I tell not actually tell an outright lie, I still felt guilty. I told them that I had been out of the country for a few years. When pressed further, I simply said, "Cherchez la femme." Technically, that was true, but not in the way my friends imagined. A few weeks before I was due to leave, I informed them that I was emigrating permanently. Naturally enough, they thought I was leaving to settle down with some woman. I organised a farewell evening when a meal in the Oliver and all drinks were on me. We had a wonderful evening. I had my American wake.

My bridge plans were also successful. I discovered that a chap I knew from Banbridge was now without a regular partner. He was happy to play with me, and we did well. We won one red point event and were placed in four others. In each year, we teamed up with two decent southern players to compete in the Holmes Wilson, finishing ninth one year and seventh in the other. Either of these top ten finishes would have taken me over my hundred red point target so I was more than happy. My only regret was that I would never find out just what Tom and I might have achieved had we stayed together for longer. I know he was very disappointed when I told him I was emigrating.

Gradually, I accumulated the books needed for the trip. Since this would be our only trip to America, we decided to bring both sets supplied to the northern bases in Britain. This meant six hundred instead of three hundred books. It was as well the spaceship had sufficient cargo space. The plan was that it would drop off one hundred and eighty at each of three locations. These bases would distribute one hundred and forty of these to other bases, making three round trips, meaning that Besil and I did not have to transport massive loads of books. The vehicle would not have been up to it. Similarly, the spaceship would distribute the clothes to the same bases.

Besil was happy enough for me to purchase the male clothing needed but insisted on taking charge of acquiring the female clothing. She took full advantage of late-night shopping in Belfast on the run up to Christmas. Darkness falling around half past four gave her over three hours in the shops. It is quite amazing what one woman can buy in that time. Three shopping trips in each winter saw her build up quite a stockpile. She declared it to be much better than her relying on my photographs. Photographs did not allow her to feel the texture of the garments.

I made arrangements with Ixos concerning my post and debit and credit cards. He would collect my post on a regular basis and read it to me. Anything where a phone call, text or email would suffice I would handle. I would need to buy a new phone once I reached the US. If a letter was required, or a form had to be completed, Ixos had access to a computer and printer in my house. He had shown himself able to reproduce my signature. In time, he might need to purchase a fresh ink cartridge, but late-night shopping in Belfast would enable that. I left him a supply of first-class stamps. I also left him the PIN for each of my cards, explaining that a new card needed to be activated using an ATM. I would not need the credit card to be sent to me. Indeed, it made sense to leave the current credit card with Ixos. Using it would enable the cash I was leaving with him to stretch further. The debit card was another matter. I would need it to be sent to me. We discussed whether it would be feasible to send it to me via Post Restante. The difficulty was that whilst we could possibly work out roughly when the card would be issued and where I would be around that time, there were all sorts of things over which we had little or no control. Suppose the Post Restante system was scrapped. What if our selected post office was closed down? It was not unknown for postal items to go astray. Ixos decided that there was nothing else to do except for him to organise the spaceship to ferry him and the card to whatever base I was visiting. I protested that this seemed an awful lot of bother just to deliver a small piece of plastic. "Not at all," said Ixos. "This project could not proceed without you or without your access to cash." His other reason was that he quite fancied a couple of visits to the US.

One other task needed to be undertaken. My knowledge of American usage of English was quite sketchy as was the case with Besil. I obtained what literature on the subject I could find, and we immersed ourselves in it. I also managed to arrange a session in the Phoenix with a chap who hailed from Kansas. He was happy to help Besil complete her purported dissertation on American English.

Finally, the big day arrived. Tatos arrived with the spaceship, and we loaded the cargo. I felt quite excited having never been to America. I found myself contrasting my journey with that undertaken by those emigrating from Ireland in the nineteenth century. I would arrive in a few short hours. They would be at sea for weeks with no guarantee of finishing the journey. Shipping losses and disease combined to claim many thousands of lives. It was a sobering thought.

The flight was smooth and uneventful. It was quite unlike any I had taken before. There was no having to check in two hours ahead of the flight, no sitting around at a crowded departure gate, and no long wait at a baggage carousel. No customs or immigration either. We were welcomed by the entire crew of the base near Washington. They had heard reports of our trips to Britain and were looking forward to getting acquainted with their American neighbours. The females mobbed Besil, each seeking to view the clothes she had brought. Apparently, pictures taken of Besil and others had prompted much admiration of the outfits worn.

The men were less interested in the male clothing. They were keen to start work on written English. However, like the women, they were looking forward to visiting the US capital. Besil and I had decided that the pattern we had followed on the last trip was the one to follow on this one also. So it was that Besil was the first Carnacan to visit an American diner. She was not impressed. "Give me Le Gavroche any time" was her comment as we strolled back to the vehicle.

I almost had cause to regret a lapse on my part. It simply had not occurred to me that Besil needed to be warned about the big difference between driving in Britain or Ireland and doing so in the US. On our first trip from the base, only quick evasive action on her part averted a head-on crash. The other driver would literally not have known what hit them because we were invisible. Besil accepted my apology, graciously telling me not to be too hard on myself. It is impossible to think of everything, was her attitude. That incident caused us to give some thought to our travel arrangements. In Britain, the distances between bases were comparatively small with only two such journeys greater than one hundred miles. The US was a different proposition. Some of the distances were close to four hundred miles. It did not seem fair that Besil should have to concentrate for long periods of time whilst I did not. I could fall asleep if I so wished. We decided that a sensible course of action would be to alternate roles when travelling between bases. Besil gave me a crash course (forgive the pun) in operating the vehicle. This was similar to driving an automatic or an electric vehicle. The vehicle was so smooth that one partially lost the sensation of speed and, initially, I had to regularly check that I was not exceeding our self-imposed speed limit.

Besil remarked about the great difference between Britain and America. In Britain, one was rarely far from a town or city. There was little real wilderness. In America, there were great swathes of open country and some really spectacular scenery. The British Isles had some beautiful countryside but little that was truly spectacular. The Slieve League Cliffs in southern Donegal, in Ireland, were about the only feature I knew which merited that adjective. But could one compare them to the Grand Canyon? America was a country of contrasts she opined – cities such as New York and vast wilderness areas, truly opulent residences and really squalid houses and apartments, multimillionaires and destitute people.

One aspect of American life provoked much comment from her. There were a great many people who were not just overweight but grossly obese. "Do they not know they are storing up health problems for later life? Do they not realise that they are shortening their life quite dramatically?" were two of her frequent remarks. I could understand her concern. I would no longer describe myself as slim but losing just half a stone from my six feet frame would leave me at my ideal weight. All of the many Carnacans I had met fitted the description of "slim." Neither Besil nor I had purchased a dress or skirt bigger than a size eight. She agreed with my suggestion that there was probably a correlation between a love of fast food and unhealthy obesity. Junk food, which was overladen with fat, sugar or salt, was a potential killer was her view. This was one aspect of human behaviour she found difficult to understand.

She was interested in the history of the North American continent. She was aware that, when the first observers had set up base, the continent was extremely sparsely populated. Indeed, the human population was outnumbered by the bison that roamed the great plains in enormous herds. The human population appeared quite different to that in Europe, and their various languages bore little resemblance to those used in Europe. These indigenous peoples had, for centuries, coexisted with nature in an admirable fashion. But major change began at the end of the fifteenth century. Europeans travelled from Britain and Europe in increasing numbers. They engaged in conflict with the native peoples and, having the benefit of more effective weaponry, defeated them and confiscated their lands. The native people were confined to small areas. The original languages were supplanted by English and Spanish, with English becoming the dominant language.

But it was not just Europeans who invaded America. Large numbers of black people arrived from Africa, although they did not appear to be doing so voluntarily. Besil listened as I recounted what I knew about the slave trade. I explained that slavery had existed on Earth as far back as recorded history. All the ancient civilisations had slave populations, be it Persia, Egypt, Greece, or Rome. Slaves, who were often captured in raids in neighbouring areas or as a result of defeat in battle, were regarded as private property and were bought and sold like other commodities. The practice never really died out but was revived in a major way between the sixteenth and nineteenth centuries. Though often portrayed as a case of whites enslaving blacks, the true picture was a bit more complex. The crews of ships involved in transporting the slaves across the Atlantic would not have been able to capture the numbers involved without local assistance. Sad to relate, many black slaves were sold into that slavery by other black people.

I related how slavery was one of the issues in dispute between the north and south in the American Civil War. Even long after that conflict, and long after the abolition of slavery, the treatment of blacks was often appalling, especially in the southern states. Even today, there are those who still regard black people as an inferior race.

Besil suggested that, whilst the horrors of total slavery were no longer to be found in most parts of the world, a milder form of slavery still existed. She cited the example of a factory owner. Two hundred people worked in his factory making shirts. Each was paid £10 per hour, earning £500 for a fifty-hour week. Each worker had a quota of shirts that they were expected to produce each week. But the owner, who did none of the work, received £5,000 per week. Was he not exploiting the workers, and was this exploitation not a form of slavery? I told her that many humans were of similar opinion and gave her a brief run-down of the political spectrum in various countries. I explained that, while other factors existed in some countries, mostly intertribal or interracial tensions, the conflict between capital and labour was universal.

The journey around the US was as much of a learning experience for me as it was for Besil and the other Carnacans. I had never been to America and had not fully realised just how different life was there when compared to Northern Ireland. Mostly, such differences were just little curiosities of no real importance. The one difference that did cause problems was language. My lessons in written English were more difficult to deliver, and progress was slower, than in Britain. In many ways, American English, especially spoken English, was a very distinct dialect. The list of items that have different names in Britain and America was long. Trash and rubbish, diaper and nappy, dumpster and skip, diner and restaurant were just a few such things. Then there were the, often irritating, usages in America, such as the ugly word "gotten." I have to admit that I frequently spoke rather disparagingly about the American version.

The trip turned out to be a greater adventure than I had anticipated. About a quarter way through our planned itinerary, we stayed at a base near Las Vegas. Behaving like typical tourists, Besil and I visited Caesar's Palace and enjoyed some time at the roulette table. Whilst there, I spotted an advert for a Texas Hold 'Em tournament, which was a qualifying event for the world championship. It was due to commence two days later. The lure was irresistible. I told Besil that I was going to enter it. After I had described the game, she opined that it seemed a much simpler game than bridge and asked that I enter her as well. I paid the $1,500 entry fee for each of us. Participants were encouraged to use a nom de plume, so she became Lethal Linnet, and I was Tiger Tony.

I realised that arriving at Caesar's Palace on the morning of the tournament would present problems. Play was due to start at 10.00 a.m. Walking from where we parked would be just too dangerous for Besil, so we arrived in the early hours, grateful that the casino was a twenty-four-hour operation. We found ourselves each sitting at one of ninety-three tables with eight players at each table. I had no idea how well either of us would do. I just hoped that neither would be eliminated at an early stage.

My tournament got off to a great start. Just a few hands in, I was holding a pair of deuces. The flop was 2, J and K all of different suits. I kept the betting reasonably low so as not to advertise my strength too early. The turn was an 8, and I did make a significant raise hoping to give a false picture of my hand. I could scarcely believe my eyes when the river gave me poker. Even better, one opponent went "all in" followed by another. We all had similar stacks, so I just followed suit. The others all folded. The first hand declared was a house of kings, which prompted the other opponent to utter an expletive as he revealed a house of jacks. The first guy's grin was short lived as I silently flipped over my cards.

That hand was a sign of things to come. Every so often, I held a hand just that bit better than that held by one or more opponents. I would beat a prial with a bigger prial, a run with a flush, a flush with a higher flush, or a house with a bigger house. I just could not go wrong. Late into the evening, the organisers called a halt to proceedings with play to resume at 10.00 the following morning. We were down to nine tables. I looked around to see if Besil was still involved. I suspected she was because, had she been eliminated, she would have come to kibbitz at my table. To my delight, she was still standing and appeared to have a really big stack.

Telling her that I would be back in a minute, I headed for a much-needed visit to the gents. Standing there, I listened to an expletive-laden tale of how he had been eliminated by "that wee bitch." He had been sitting with a pair of bullets. The table was AH, AS, 6C, 9C, and 10C. Both of them had good stacks with hers just slightly bigger. Inevitably, the betting finished with him going "all in." The "bitch" came up with 7C and 8C for a straight flush, wiping him out. "She is not natural," he declared.

"She has the best poker face I have ever seen. She does not need dark glasses and has no physical tells whatsoever. I just could not read her." Just as it was dawning on me that he was talking about Besil, he finished by saying that she certainly lived up to the lethal appellation. I took great pleasure in retailing this rant to Besil. She accepted my praise in a matter-of-fact manner and confirmed, to my relief, that she had not employed any mind-reading techniques.

We stayed inside the casino dozing in armchairs. The following morning, we resumed play. By now, I was hoping that one or other of us would survive until the final three tables. Prize money went down to twenty fourth, although below twentieth, one would just have the entry fee refunded. My good luck continued to hold up, and, in due course, I found myself at one of the four remaining tables, with Besil one of my opponents. It soon became clear that the sore loser's description of Besil was accurate. She was simply unreadable, and she knew how to exploit that advantage. After winning two hands with good hands, she pulled off quite a coup on the next. The table had a pair of tens and three other unrelated cards. After the river was exposed, she piled in with a massive bet. Her two remaining opponents both folded, each saying, "My other small pair won't count." Although not required to, Besil exposed her cards showing that she had just the pair on the table. A brilliant bluff.

I was lucky enough to stay out of the action at that table. Once she had eliminated five of our opponents, we were dispersed to other tables and did not meet up again until the final table. She had, by far, the biggest stack and knew how to use it to her advantage. A couple of times, she effectively bullied opponents out of pots. As might be expected, the others at the table were all seasoned campaigners and formidable opponents. Even so, one by one, they fell afoul of Lethal Linnet until just one remained at the table with Besil and me. Next came my turn as, in the space of two hands, she eliminated me with the same dispassionate efficiency. By now, the organisers were playing "Another one bites the dust" at each elimination. It actually felt quite humiliating, even though I knew most competitors would have been delighted to go as deep as I had. The $30,000 prize money helped ease the pain. Besil was expressionless as she despatched her last opponent. There followed the presentation of the trophy and her prize money, thankfully all in cash. When interviewed by a reporter from a local television station, she was asked about how long she had been playing the game. She calmly stated that the tournament had been the first time she had ever played poker. Needless to say, this was dismissed by all present as another bluff by Lethal Linnet.

We had both qualified for the world championship, which was just nine weeks away. No way were we going to miss out on that, so our stay near Vegas would last a little longer. Back at the base, we were surprised to receive a communication from Ixos. Besil's triumph had made not just network television in the US but had also been reported by Sky and the BBC. Even I had got a mention. Initially, the general view was that this diminutive Irish woman had been spoofing about her lack of experience. But a little research had revealed no trace of her in any poker competition either live or online. On hearing this, I expressed concern that media attention might pose problems. Any invented background story would easily be revealed as false. We decided that Lethal Linnet would just have to be Mystery Woman Lethal Linnet and refuse to divulge any personal information. That might drive the media mad, but the organisers and their sponsors would be delighted with the blaze of publicity.

Ixos also mentioned that a new debit card had arrived, which he had already activated. He hoped to travel over soon with Tatos. Pointing out that such a journey was now unnecessary, because we now had an unexpected $140,000 available, made no difference to his plans. Clearly, he had no notion of missing out on a visit to America.

Our arrival at Caesar's nine weeks later was very different from that for the qualifying tournament. The first time, we had been two unknown competitors who attracted zero attention. Whilst Besil had drawn attention even at an early stage, I was only noticed when I reached the latter stages. This time, it was virtually impossible to find a quiet corner. Besil was definitely the flavour of the month, and she was plagued with requests for interviews, all of which she refused. Her line was that she needed to gather her concentration before play started. Prior to play starting, any competitor who had previously won the tournament was introduced to the room. Once all such had been named, the MC declared that he was waiting to see whether all of these great champions would be eclipsed by the new star in world poker, Lethal Linnet.

Sitting down to play, I felt strangely calm. This was in contrast to the nervousness I always felt prior to a bridge competition. I suppose this was down to the realisation that bridge and poker were so very different. There was some skill involved in poker, but this was dwarfed by the amount of luck involved. By contrast, while there was a small element of luck with bridge, one's finishing position always reflected the performance put in by one's partner and oneself.

Early elimination seemed a real possibility during the first hour of play. A couple of decent hands running into a couple of better hands left me in real peril. Playing short stacked is never much fun, and there is the temptation to throw caution to the wind and bet recklessly. I sought to continue to play normally, and gradually my situation improved. The hours passed, and, at the close of play that evening, I felt tired but also relieved to still be in the competition. My situation was nowhere nearly as good as during qualifying, but I was still there. As I made my way over to the table where Besil was gathering up her chips, I could see that she had enjoyed a much better session. I doubted that any other player had a bigger stack.

My fortunes changed for the better the following day. Lady luck really smiled on me, and my stack grew rapidly. I even managed to make a dent in Besil's stack when I filled a flush with the river to beat her run. In due course, we both took our seats at the final table. I was the second of the eight to depart with my house of sixes losing out to Besil's well-hidden house of sevens.

There was simply no stopping her, and that night, she lifted the trophy and a cool million dollars. Still, her demeanour remained unchanged. The media attention was unbelievable, with even *Vogue* expressing an interest in poker for the first time ever. The organisers were truly delighted and very keen to get an assurance from Besil that she would return the following year to defend her title. They also passed on to her congratulatory messages from both the First Minister and Deputy First Minister, the Taoiseach, Uachtarán na hÉireann and the UK Prime Minister. While she could refuse to give interviews, she was unable to prevent photographs and film footage being shot. As a consequence, during the rest of our trip, she was recognised wherever we went. It was weird to receive complimentary drinks wherever we went, considering she had just won $1 million. Even my seventh-place prize of $50,000 was not insignificant.

The crew at the base all wished to visit the scene of Besil's triumphs. We taught each of them how to play Hold 'Em and explained how roulette operated. Instead, the $4,000 we had intended to leave at the base, we left $104,000 so that each crew member would have $5,000 with which to visit the casino. If they all displayed the same poker skills as Besil, the poker players they would encounter were in for a hard time. Throughout the rest of the trip, we received periodic reports of large amounts of cash won by various crew members. As the cash accumulated, that crew asked for advice on what to do with it. They could only spend relatively small amounts. They readily accepted my suggestion that they donate some to charity. So, it was that various organisations found an envelope containing $10,000 in their letter box with a note that said, "Put this to good use."

We received a laconic communication from Citas that said, "I only get £20 when I win the whist."

Our mood was relaxed as I drove the vehicle away from the base near Vegas heading westwards. As we crossed the desert, Besil entertained me by singing a selection of songs. After a couple of hours, we stopped for a snack, and I took the opportunity to leave the vehicle for a comfort break. I was wearing a tennis shirt, shorts and open sandals. Just as I was finishing, I felt an intense pain in my left calf. I had been bitten by a snake. When I was about halfway back to the vehicle, everything went black.

When I awoke, I was in a bed in a dimly lit room. "Welcome back" was the greeting from a Carnacan in the room. He turned up the lighting using a dimmer switch and proceeded to check my temperature, pulse and blood pressure. I had many questions and learnt that I had collapsed fifteen yards away from the vehicle. At risk to her own well-being, Besil left the sanctuary of the vehicle and braved the blazing sunshine to half-carry and half-drag me to the vehicle. She then drove at top speed to the base we were bound for as it was the closest. On the way, she alerted the base to the situation enabling their medical specialist to prepare to treat me. On arrival, I was very close to death. It was estimated that ten minutes later, I might have been beyond help. I had lain unconscious for nine days. It was only during the past forty-eight hours that the medic had become confident I would survive. Throughout those days, Besil had rarely left my bedside other than to snatch a couple of hours of rest. She was sleeping at present.

So steadfast had been her vigil that she refused to travel back to Vegas to defend her title. Instead, she sent Patil in her place. The two were very alike and it was most unlikely the substitution would be detected. Patil played her part well, refusing all requests for interviews. She also played her poker well, finishing a very creditable third bringing back a prize of $200,000, most of which was donated over time to charity.

I found the reunion with Besil very emotional. "I owe you my life," I told her. Her response surprised me. "Now the debt is finally repaid," she said. She was referring to the occasion when Mickey McAteer had saved Citas's life. The crew at the base had felt in debt to Mickey. Besil was delighted that she had been able not just to help save me but also to repay the debt to humanity.

I spent a further two days confined to bed and a further four at the base before Besil agreed that we continue our journey. It was as well that I no longer had any reason to rush back to

Knocknashee. My encounter with the snake had added almost three years to the trip. Who knew how long it would be before I saw Newry again? What was certain was that I had no great desire for any further excitement. Little did I know what was just around the corner.

When we arrived, the crew at the base in Washington State, seemed much less calm than would have been normal. It was not our visit that was disturbing them. Baros simply stated, "World War Three is under way." This was a bolt from the blue. Of course, I had been aware of long-standing tensions between Russia and NATO; military skirmishes in Africa, involving Russian and Chinese forces; and increasing hostility between China and the US. But there had been no indication that outright war was imminent. Still, thinking back, September 11th had come as a complete shock to most of us. Clearly, some incident must have triggered hostilities.

Strangely, my first thoughts were about my Carnacan friends. "Does this mean ye will be leaving Earth?" I asked. Baros assured me that it did not. "We are quite safe within our bases unless a nuclear bomb detonates within a half-mile of the barrier." He added, "You are safer here than taking a leak in the desert." Despite his deadpan expression, I thought this was another example of a Carnacan developing a sense of humour. When I asked whether any bases had been damaged, he revealed that two bases, one in Russia and one in China, had suffered damage. In neither case had anyone been hurt, but in each case, the barrier had been breached with no chance of repair. This had rendered the time dilator inoperable so, whilst the base was still inhabitable, it was no longer desirable to use it. Doing so would cause the crew to age prematurely. Accordingly, they were in the process of evacuating to the base in Antarctica. This was not a straightforward operation because they wished to remove all traces of Carnacan activity from each base including all of the damaged barrier. Removing the equipment from inside the base was the simpler part. The barrier was not so easy. They could only work on it during the hours of darkness without the benefit of artificial light.

It was a short-lived war often described by later historians as the Four Ps war. Before describing the course of that war, it is best to consider the various developments that led to its eruption. None of these developments would have been sufficient in itself to precipitate worldwide conflict, so it was unfortunate for humanity that they all occurred within the same time period.

The first P was Putin. The belligerent military posturing by Putin that began in 2014 created a state of tension between Russia and NATO. For the most part, this was centred on the border between Ukraine and Russia, but there was also tension between Russia and the Baltic states of Latvia, Lithuania, and Estonia. Commentators are divided on Putin's motives and intentions. Some believe he wished to recreate the former Soviet Union, and there is some evidence that he felt his role as President of Russia was greatly diminished from that enjoyed by previous Soviet leaders, such as Stalin and Kruschev. Apparently, the name Gorbachev was totally anathema to Putin as he blamed the introduction of glasnost and perestroika for the downfall of the Soviet Union.

After amassing a vast army on the Ukrainian border, he invaded. Had he assembled his forces quickly and invaded immediately, he could well have succeeded albeit with significant losses on both sides. Indeed, initially it appeared he would succeed but, with increased military supplies from the West, Ukraine was able to turn the tide. They regained all the territory with a Ukrainian-speaking majority before a truce was agreed. In reality, it was less of a truce than an armed standoff.

Another school of thought held that Putin was less interested in the recreation of a Russian empire, or even the advancement of Russian interests, but in his own personal aggrandisement. He envied the absolute control exercised by Stalin. Certainly, some of his behaviour resembled that of a megalomaniac who liked playing with toy soldiers. A review of events in Russia in the late 2020s and early 2030s supports this view. Once the Russian public grew bored with him continuing to issue empty threats over Ukraine and other matters, he decided he needed to open up another front. His allies in intelligence framed three of his principal opponents in the Politburo, implicating them in an alleged coup attempt. A show trial followed in which the three and several others were convicted of treason and executed. Putin sought and was awarded sweeping new powers. Effectively, he became an absolute dictator with the right to appoint a deputy who would succeed him in the role. Unsurprisingly, he nominated a person whom many suspected was his illegitimate son. A further demonstration of his mindset was his decree that he be known as Putin the First, while his son would become Putin the Second. Perhaps it was not Stalin but the Czars he wished to emulate.

If the world thought the situation would improve after Putin's death, they were sorely disappointed. Putin 2 was cut from the same mould as his predecessor. If anything, he was more dangerous as he lacked the native cunning the former possessed. Certainly, many think that had Putin 1 still been in charge, relations with China would not have deteriorated in the way they did.

For a couple of decades, China had used the fruits of its tremendous economic growth to extend its influence in the world. Their efforts were mainly focussed on Africa where government-controlled companies made significant investments in various countries. Often, such investments were accompanied by soft loans. This activity created some alarm both in the West and in Russia. It was obvious that it was a matter of when, not if, China overtook the US as the world's largest economy. If China also had the support of many client states in Africa, it would replace the US as the world's alpha male.

But, to quote Robbie Burns, "The best laid plans of mice and men so often gang agley." One African state experienced a change of government following a major scandal involving the previous ruling party. Part of the scandal involved the receipt of backhanders by government ministers. That money was Chinese. As a result, the new government was vehemently anti-Chinese. It nationalised all businesses funded by Chinese investment without compensation and refused to make any further repayments on the substantial debt owed to China. Retaliation was quick. China sent a significant number of troops to an adjacent client state, claiming its assistance had been requested to counter an alleged threat of invasion.

The first state made frantic representations to the US, seeking protection. They were out of luck. The humiliation suffered during the withdrawal from Afghanistan was still fresh in the American psyche and no president, Democrat or Republican, was going to embark on another overseas mission. Putin 2 saw an opportunity for glory and offered to provide troops. His offer was accepted. Subsequent months saw border skirmishes in which both Russian and Chinese troops were involved. Sino-Russian relations worsened even further when a third African state first invited in Russian troops and then nationalised Chinese interests.

Many observers were surprised that, despite recent history, the US did not accede to the request for assistance. While there had not been any military threat from either to the other, there existed a de facto state of economic war between the two countries. For years, the Chinese government had sponsored an espionage programme. Intellectual property belonging to American and European companies was plundered. Doubtless, this ill-gained knowledge helped to short circuit what might otherwise have been a lengthy research and development programme and contributed to China's rapid economic advance. Surely, the US should have availed of an opportunity to put a spoke in China's wheel.

There could well have been a very different response had those African episodes occurred a couple of years later when the political landscape had altered dramatically. In 2024, Joe Biden surprised many when he expressed a wish to serve a second term. Given his age and questions concerning his memory and mental acuity, the hierarchy of the Democrats were not especially keen but could not see any way to prevent it without risking splitting the party. Besides, it looked as though the Republicans were going to have a messy season of primaries with that party deeply split between the pro- and anti-Trump factions. The Republican was fractious in the extreme but, in spite of deep splits, the party rallied around the chosen candidate. The Republican cause was greatly assisted by revelations that emerged during the week before polling of certain business dealings by Biden's son. Thus, eight years of Republican presidency followed.

2032 saw the rapid rise of Marco Benedetti, a Democratic senator of Italian extraction. He was just fifty years old, handsome, charismatic, silver tongued, and widowed three years earlier. He was a shoe-in as a presidential candidate. Like Biden before him, he chose a black woman as his running mate. This time, she was also lesbian and a prominent advocate of LBGTQ+ rights. In truth, he would have won with a statue as running mate, so the landslide victory was not unexpected.

Just over halfway through his term of office, he lost his life in a car crash. While most of the nation was plunged into genuine mourning, others were of a different mind. They had put up with a black president with Obama, but in no way would the Ku Klux Clan tolerate a black lesbian as POTUS. As she stood beside Benedetti's grave in Arlington Cemetery, she was hit in the head by a sniper's bullet.

Although the nation was shocked, both politicians and the public went about their business as normal. Presidential assassination was not unknown in the US, and the rules of succession were well established. Political equilibrium might have been maintained were it not for events that occurred just three weeks later. A group of four Islamic extremists managed to evade security and enter the chamber in the House of Representatives. Two opened fire with submachine guns whilst the others threw hand grenades. Then all four detonated suicide vests. The result was carnage. Seventy-nine congressmen died in the chamber. Seventeen others were rushed to the hospital with severe injuries. Of these, nine died during the following fortnight.

As if that were not bad enough, another group carried out a simultaneous attack on the trading floor of the Stock Exchange on Wall Street in New York. Here, the death toll was not as great given that the heyday of open outcry trading had long passed. Indeed, the attack was largely symbolic as computer trading carried on without disruption.

Coming so soon after the death of both the President and Vice President, these atrocities were enough to spur the military into action. The new President readily agreed that martial law be declared, and the country found itself under the control of a quinquevirate, consisting of the chiefs of the Army, Navy and Air Force together with the heads of the CIA and FBI. It was planned that his group would remain in charge for five years. Elections for half of the seats in Congress would be held two years later followed by the rest two years after that. This would be essentially a shadow Congress with powers not being restored to the elected representatives until a President was elected twelve months later. Had these five been in charge when the request for help came from Africa, the Russians would never have had the opportunity to establish a foothold.

Inevitably, with the military in charge, foreign policy became much more hawkish. Proactive measures were instituted not just to combat Chinese espionage but to turn the situation into more of a two-way street. Large numbers of computer-savvy people were recruited to beef up defences against cyberattacks. The energies of some of these people were diverted into areas other than such defence.

So, it was in 2038 that the world could have been described as a tinderbox. It would not take much of a spark to ignite a conflict. But that spark arrived in a rather unexpected manner. The military standoff on the border between Russia and Ukraine had persisted for more than a decade. Complacency had set in on both sides as had a certain ennui. Bored troops will always find some form of diversion, and, for some, this diversion took the form of smuggling operations. Contacts had been established between some Ukrainian forces and their Russian counterparts. The main traffic was from Ukraine to Russia with the chief commodities being western goods not easily obtained in Russia and various class A drugs. One of those involved on the Russian side was Dimitri Karpov, who commanded an artillery battery. One evening, he was awaiting the delivery of a large consignment that required the use of a forty-ton lorry.

The lorry driver encountered problems en route. Before he reached the border, one of his front tyres was punctured. The second P. Cursing his luck, he and his mate went to change the wheel only to find that the jack had been ditched, possibly to leave more room for cargo. Either that or it had been stolen and sold on. His efforts to pass on the bad news to the Brigadier running the operation failed because he kept being diverted to voicemail. The brigadier was busy enjoying the delights of the third P, a local prostitute with his phone switched off.

On the other side of the border, Dimitri was becoming more and more incensed. Bad faith was rare in these cross-border transactions but not totally unknown. His ill humour was increased by the fact that this was the biggest deal he had ever made, and he had paid sixty per cent of the price up front. To enable him to make that advance payment, he had needed to borrow a huge amount from the Russian mafia group who would distribute the goods and drugs. If he could not produce the goods or repay the money, life could become very difficult. He had tried ringing that Ukrainian brigadier but was diverted to voicemail. Had Dimitri been thinking clearly, he might have waited a little longer before acting. But he had consumed a significant quantity of vodka and was quite drunk.

His order to fire the various artillery pieces surprised his men but such was his reputation for administering condign punishment to those who crossed him that they obeyed. The Ukrainian positions, which came under attack were equally surprised and replied in kind, without seeking authorisation from the higher command. The exchange of fire spread right along the front.

Matters might have been contained had the fourth P not intervened. The Pentagon decided to seize the moment. They had few real worries concerning Russia, but China was a different matter. China had already exceeded the US economically and was catching up militarily. The US could defeat the Chinese now, but in ten or fifteen years, the result might be different. Logic dictated that they take them on sooner rather than later. As it happened, though, they did not need to take on the task themselves. The Russians would do it for them.

One of the fruits of their efforts in cyberspace was control of the Russian military's computer systems. It was a simple matter to launch a fleet of thirty-five Russian nuclear missiles towards Chinese cities. To muddy the waters, and provide justification for their next move, they launched another one towards Hawaii but altered its trajectory so that it would plunge into the ocean some fifty miles short. The resulting tidal wave might cause some damage, but things needed to look realistic.

Immediately following these launches, the Pentagon crashed the military computer system together with all Russian telephone systems, effectively preventing any coordinated action by Russia. They used a hotline to tell the Chinese that Russia had attacked both countries. They would be retaliating against Russia but hoped China would not follow the Russian example. The plan worked. The Chinese fired all that they had at Russia, adding to the massive damage caused by the heavy American bombardment.

It did not really matter whether the Chinese really believed the Americans. They were nothing but pragmatic. By the time they finished talking to them, many cities were in ruins and around two hundred million of their citizens had perished with many more to die from injuries and radiation sickness in the coming weeks. Fighting the US would be foolhardy in any circumstance. Starting from an already weakened position would be lunacy especially as the US appeared to be unaffected so far. They had been monitoring the American media and, other than Hawaii, the US had shipped no damage. Perhaps the intelligence, which suggested that the US had breached arms control treaties by developing anti-ballistic defence systems, had underestimated the progress made. What they did know was that they could not afford to be hit by a fleet of missiles fired by the US in addition to whatever else the Russians might send.

The Russians did manage to fire a handful of missiles towards the US, but they were ineffective. The US did have an anti-ballistic missile screen. It would have been unable to cope with a full-scale attack, but it dealt with the few that were fired, preventing any from reaching American soil. So badly was Russia hit from both of the other superpowers that, when the US, after allowing the resumption of telephone communication, ordered them to cease the attack on Ukraine, they complied.

The top brass in the Pentagon were elated. In the space of two days, they had eliminated the threat from both major adversaries without incurring any American casualties of significant damage to American property. China would take decades to recover whilst Russia would probably never fully recover. Under normal circumstances, they would have been feted for such a miraculous feat. But they had to keep the detail of their operations under wraps. What they had done amounted to mass murder and would be a war crime in anybody's book. All records alluding in any way to the hacking of the Russian computer system and the operation itself were given the highest security classification and sealed for one hundred and fifty years.

Of course, there were those who harboured doubts about the official version put out by the Pentagon. This was that they had detected the launches aimed at China and Hawaii and, fearing the next wave would be heading their way, had managed to knock out the Russian command system. The method used could not be revealed without endangering state security. Of course, the Russians disputed this version but faced the difficulty of explaining how their missiles were launched. Add in that there was clear evidence that they had initiated, without any hint of provocation, the artillery exchanges on their Ukrainian border, and they were never going to be believed.

Outside of the Pentagon and those directly involved, I was the only human who knew the full truth. This was only because the Carnacans had been able to monitor various communications and pieced the truth together.

One Carnacan thought there was a further truth that needed to be uncovered. "Had we left," Besil asked, "would you have come with us to Carnac or stayed on Earth?" It was a valid question. The answer might have depended on just how quickly they had gone. If I had been compelled to decide before the outcome was known, I would almost certainly have left with them. By knowing how it had happened, the decision would be more finely balanced. Would I really cut myself off completely from humanity and my native planet? I was not sure.

Chapter 9

During the weeks following the short-lived conflict, the world was preoccupied with inquests into events. Throughout the globe, there was a genuine sense of shock at the number of casualties. Given that some cities in both China and Russia had effectively ceased to exist, only the broadest estimate of the number of those killed or seriously injured was possible. The final estimate for Chinese deaths was around three hundred and eighty million. The Russian figure was one hundred and fifteen million. This represented some six per cent of the global population killed within two days. Had Russia been able to fire its full arsenal of nuclear weapons, deaths in the US and Europe could have doubled the casualty list. Non-nuclear countries were appalled. In any previous conflict, they could mount some sort of defence against an aggressor or go to the aid of an ally under attack. But the conflict had revealed the true extent of their powerlessness.

I got the impression that the Carnacans were totally shocked by what they had witnessed. One said that the death toll was not as bad as had occurred in the pandemic on Carnac but, in one respect, it was worse. Deaths from their pandemic had been unavoidable. Humanity's recent death toll was self-inflicted. I could not argue with that judgement.

Somehow a lot of the joy had gone from my life. I had not been directly affected by the conflict. I knew many in the US, Western Europe and other parts of the globe were singing Te Deums in their relief that their country had been spared. Instead of relief, I felt a sense of shame that my friends had seen humanity at its worst. Besil seemed to sense my mood. Repeatedly, she told me that I should not blame myself. The war had not been my fault. Gradually, her efforts bore fruit, and I found myself enjoying life again.

I investigated the bridge scene in the US, and Besil and I rejigged the remainder of our trip to facilitate our participation in several important competitions. There is not a big overlap between the bridge and poker worlds. Even so, we did come to media attention after we won both the second and third events we entered after coming a close second to two regulars on the US team in our first event. Our successes did not go unnoticed back in Ireland. I had been NIBU Chairman and IBU President, and some of my bridge friends were still alive. Several congratulatory emails arrived. I also received an email from the *Irish Bridge Journal,* for whom I had supplied reports on the northern bridge scene over a three-year period. They wanted to do a piece on this nonagenarian who was conquering the bridge scene in the US. I did reply cooperatively. I waxed lyrical on how I had, in my later years, discovered on how to concentrate properly. I added that Besil Linnet was by far and away the best partner I ever had. Quite deliberatively, I was vague about how we had met and provided very little by way of biographical detail for her.

The article in the IBJ was republished in the *Irish Times*, which had run a weekly bridge column for many years. I had often competed against its columnist, John Comyn, who was now deceased. I did not know the present columnist, but it seemed they had been playing schools bridge when I was IBU President. The *Irish Times* coverage prompted reports on RTE, BBC NI, and UTV. These came to the attention of Knocknashee, prompting Ixos to send a communication. This contained congratulations but concluded with a question. "Is Besil a better bridge partner than me?" I did not know whether he was expressing some form of annoyance or just taking the quote from me at face value. Whichever it was, he had a point.

I realised that it might be unwise to attract any more media attention on either side of the Atlantic. The more that journalists or reporters enquired into Besil's background, the greater the likelihood that the absence of any record of her existence prior to her bursting onto the poker scene would be uncovered. There was also the danger that somebody would compare photographs taken back then with how she looked now. Whilst some people aged well, her lack of aging was very obvious. And the same applied to me. I was rapidly closing in on the ton in terrestrial years but still looked like a man in his sixties.

So, for the remainder of the trip, we tried to keep a low profile. Besil had a lifetime exemption from having to qualify for the world poker championship but did not attend again. The next time, I emailed the organisers informing them that Lethal Linnet was ill, and we stayed out of human sight for several weeks. The following year we did not even do that; we just lay low.

However, there arose one temptation that I found irresistible. A report in *The New York Times* mentioned an upcoming sudoku competition sponsored by a Japanese multinational company. Qualifiers were being held all over the US with the final in New York a few weeks later. I had taken part in such a competition in London back in the noughties. It had been organised by *Daily Telegraph* columnist David Mepham, who had been the person to introduce the Japanese puzzle to the UK. Around two hundred people had taken part in the final, which was held in the Masons' Arms. I had finished thirteenth. I expected Besil to show a great aptitude for sudoku, which requires a logical approach and an ability to carry mental operations through a number of stages. I was not disappointed.

In the qualifier, one had to solve three puzzles, each of which would be rated "super fiendish." A half-hour was allowed for each. I scraped through, while Besil surprised everyone by completing each puzzle in around fifteen minutes. She was handed a cheque for $250. This she retained as a souvenir, lacking the documentation needed for opening a bank account. The final, for which around four hundred had qualified, followed a similar pattern. This time, there were five puzzles of even greater difficulty. I actually managed to complete one of them, which boosted my final standing to seventeenth. Besil completed all puzzles with ease. Another souvenir cheque.

Her feat was front-page news in *The New York Times* with the headline, "Lethal Linnet Strikes Again." We definitely needed to lie low for a while. We did not even venture out to celebrate my hundredth birthday even though we were now in Canada where the media coverage had been much less intense. Birthday celebrations did not occur on Carnac. Only two events were celebrated there. One was the end of education bringing the start of public service, effectively a twenty-fifth birthday celebration. The other was the end of public service and start of retirement, a fiftieth birthday. But the crew at the base and Besil entered into the spirit of things. They acquired drinks, including champagne from a local store. Each handed me a birthday card and applauded as I blew out the hundred candles on the cake. I had tears in my eyes as Besil sang, "Happy Birthday."

Looking back, I think I was homesick. Not so much homesick for any particular place but homesick for my previous normal human existence. I may have had contact with waiters, barmen, shopkeepers, and others during my time in America and Canada, but it was as an outsider. I longed for the feeling of belonging that I enjoyed growing up in Armagh, during married life in Newcastle, whilst living near Dunleer and later in Newry. I missed being part of the bridge community in Ireland. I missed hearing, "Well Tony, how goes it?" We were due to return to Knocknashee after just two more base visits, but it would not feel like returning home. After an absence of almost forty years, I would be arriving as a stranger. My friends would all be dead. My sons, if still alive, would be old men, and older in appearance than me. Even Newry would be greatly changed. In addition to the normal gradual process of change, there had been a major redevelopment involving a new park, civic centre and relief road.

I was reminded of my mother describing how she felt homesick one New Year's Eve. During the evening, a local band gave a performance in the street near her house. She had been reared in Salford and had moved to Warrenpoint when my father changed jobs. She had been married for six years and had three young children. Her father had died during her teens from wounds and damage from being gassed while serving as a stretcher bearer during the Great War. Her mother had died three years after my mother's marriage. The band struck up, "Home sweet home." My mother told how she wept for the home she missed, a home that no longer existed. I now knew how she must have felt.

When we eventually arrived back at Knocknashee, a visit to Newry confirmed that things were just as I had expected. All of my drinking pals in the Phoenix were dead. Similarly, only one member of any of the three local bridge clubs had survived. Many of the shops and businesses in the town were different. Ixos had already informed me that the vacant lot near my house had been developed. This prompted me into a move. Even without my poker winnings, my personal wealth had grown substantially. In total, I was worth just shy of a million pounds. A house less than half a mile from Knocknashee was on the market. Further enquiries revealed it had been up for sale for almost a year. So, it was not surprising that the vendor accepted my offer immediately. I suspect it must have been one of the fastest completions on record.

My landlord's son, who had inherited the property, seemed surprisingly happy when I gave him three months' notice of my intention to move out. It transpired that he was thinking of selling the house, and he reckoned it was better to do so without a sitting tenant.

I also purchased a workshop on Kilmorey Street, which had a large yard. This would guarantee the crew and I the use of a safe parking space during any visits to Newry. I swear that Ixos almost smiled when he saw the legend I had placed over the entrance to the yard. It read "Carnac Developments."

I did receive one pleasant surprise. During my stays at Knocknashee and the trips to Britain and America, Besil had been kind enough to trim my hair when asked to do so, and she did a reasonable job. One afternoon I went into Goldilocks, the hairdressing salon I had used prior to my absences from Newry. The two chairs were occupied, and one of the stylists came over to greet me at the counter. I enquired about an appointment either that afternoon or the following day. At this, one of the customers turned round and exclaimed, "It can't be, can it? It is you, Tony?" I did not recognise her until she said she was Sarah, and the two stylists were her daughters, Esme and Jesse. Sarah was the daughter of the original salon owner, Janet. She had been in her twenties when she worked with Janet in the early nineties. Now retired, she retained ownership of the salon with the business firmly in family hands.

This was the first occasion on which I was quizzed in depth on how I managed to look so young and have such a good head of hair. "But if I remember right, you were a few years older than mammy. You must be over a hundred," Sarah said. She even speculated on me being my son impersonating his father. She kept repeating that I did not look a day older than she remembered me around fifty years earlier. This was the sort of conversation to which I became accustomed as time passed.

The reason I had given my landlord three months' notice instead of the one to which he was entitled was that my new house required some renovation. I organised local tradesmen to replaster the internal walls, install underfloor heating powered by a heat pump, new wooden flooring, and a jacuzzi. The promise of bonuses for prompt completion ensured the work was completed inside three weeks. The plasterer assured me that the old rule that one should not paint plastered walls for at least six months no longer applied with modern plasters. Six weeks of drying time was ample, he reckoned. I could do it more quickly if I kept the heat on and hired a couple of dehumidifiers.

My original intention was to hire a professional painter. Besil suggested I do the decorating myself because she would like to assist me. It would give her another experience of human life. I was happy to agree even though it caused me to reorder my plans. Remembering that the stuff from the barriers around the two bases abandoned during the war was in storage at the Antarctic base, I had outlined to Ixos how I wanted to create a truly unique house. He had agreed readily.

The spaceship arrived with its cargo and four of the crew spent two nights helping me clad my house with stuff. Once that was finished, Magas tweaked the settings so that the house was visible. My need for the house to be seen contrasted with the Carnacan need for an undetectable base. A time dilator was the first item of furnishings installed. Had I employed a painter, this work would have had to wait until he finished. With Besil looking to spend a lot of time in the house, I wanted it to be a slow-time-speed zone for obvious reasons. Using brochures and stuff downloaded from the internet, Besil helped me choose colour schemes, furniture and curtains. It felt great working in partnership, reminding me of time spent in Dunleer over fifty years earlier.

The BT engineers had looked at me as if my head was cut when I requested that they install a WiFi hub in the shed. They still were not totally convinced it was a good idea even after I had spun the yarn that I was going to convert the shed into an office. But I got what I wanted. Installing the hub in the house would have presented problems with the cladding I was not sure I could solve.

The painting and decorating progressed well with Besil being not the only Carnacan helping out. Looking back, I believe that every crew member contributed something to the work. I was delighted with the outcome. Once the house was ready, I organised my house-warming. All of the crew attended, although four of them had to miss an hour of the party so as to ensure the base was not left unmanned. Thankfully, we did not have to worry about the neighbours. The nearest house was two hundred yards away. It was occupied by an elderly woman who was something of a recluse. No other house was within four hundred yards. During the evening, I unveiled the plaque showing the name I had chosen for the house, which was *Domhain Eile*, which means Other World.

I told the Carnacans to treat the house as an extension to the base, and most took advantage of my offer. Their enthusiasm was not hard to understand. For over three hundred terrestrial years, they had been cooped up inside the base with only the occasional trip outside during which trips they were confined to the vehicle. During the past fifty years or so, they had enjoyed the occasional visit to Newry. The house was a kind of halfway house. Instead of the artificial light in the underground base, they could enjoy natural daylight whilst still enjoying the protection of the barrier enclosing the house.

I still spent some time in the base continuing tuition in written English, but the majority of my time was spent in the house. I had no idea of how future events would unfold, but I thought that I should make a start on writing this chronicle. It might never be read by anyone else, but I felt I should put things on the record whilst I was able. Living in slow-time speed would not necessarily protect me from debilitating illness or, worse still, dementia. Given my experience of Besil's performances in poker, bridge, and sudoku, I thought there was little point in introducing her to chess. I thought I might have a better chance of beating her at Scrabble. I did win the games we played on the first evening. But I made the mistake of leaving the Official Scrabble Dictionary on one of the bookshelves. Her capacity for total recall did the rest, and I found myself on the wrong end of some serious drubbings. Had she entered any official championships, I would not have given her opponents much chance. It was a pity we could not risk her entering for fear of attracting too much media interest in Lethal Linnet.

In many ways, they were blissful times. I had no financial worries. I might not have much human contact, but the Carnacans were pleasant companions, especially Besil. If I thought about it, I realised I was totally in love with her. Continually, I had to remind myself that any attempt by me to move our relationship into something more than friendship would be both unfair and selfish. Doubtless, if asked, Besil would have sexual relations with me but any pleasure to be derived would be totally one-sided. I should count myself fortunate to have such a beautiful, intelligent and friendly companion who seemed happy to spend a great deal of time with me.

Having brushed up my O Level French, and learnt a little German, Spanish, and Italian, Besil and I undertook a couple of brief trips to bases in Europe. Whilst we were not directly affected, travel for humans had become a lot simpler. The days of long delays at airport security and restrictions on what could be taken on board had gone. This was as a result of action taken by the American quinquevirate. The horrendous casualty figures in China and Russia had shocked most of humanity into a more peaceable existence. Events on the Russian-Ukrainian border had revealed that serious conflict could be triggered by accident. There was also the determination on the part of various governments to grow their economies by taking advantage of the wiping out of much of Chinese industrial capacity. Countries such as the US, India, Korea, and Vietnam were the main beneficiaries. But even sclerotic economies, such as Japan, Germany, and France felt some benefit.

There remained one fly in the ointment. Islamic terrorism. Ever since September 11, intelligence services and special forces from western countries had conducted operations to identify, locate, and destroy terrorist operatives. There had always been a realisation that a piecemeal degradation of the various terrorist organisations was never going to be successful. Take out one member or one leader, and another will take his place. Nor was it possible to address the root causes of the problem. There might be some jihadists whose motivation was their interpretation, however warped, of the Quran, but, for many, the motivation was much more political. They saw how oil and other resources, which should have helped provide a better life for millions of people, had instead been exploited by western companies and a small ruling elite.

One jihadist organisation had been behind the attacks on the House of Representatives and the New York Stock Exchange. It regarded these attacks as being even more successful as September 11. The death toll might have been much lower, but the effect had been greater. They had destroyed, temporarily at least, democratic government in the US. Who knows what another such attack might achieve. Even if it just postponed the resumption of American democracy, it would be viewed as successful. The target and timing were each very symbolic. Mass in St Patrick's Cathedral on March 17 saw the church

crowded with several senior Democrats of Irish descent in attendance. The attack by six men, using submachine guns, grenades, and, finally, suicide vests left almost nine hundred dead
and many more seriously injured. The outrage spread well beyond the US. This was not just an attack on America but one
on Christian worship. Even the Irish government declared its
willingness to abandon its long-held policy of neutrality and
provide troops to partake in a coalition campaign against the
jihadists.

The quinquevirate surprised the world with its response. It
was a response no democratic politician could ever have made.
It began with a request that Al Qaeda, Isis, and all other Islamic
groups publicly declare an end to jihad. It continued by publishing details of an aid programme to Afghanistan costing in excess of $45 billion. That country had suffered economic collapse
and famine during the years that had followed the withdrawal
of American troops and the restoration of government by the
Taliban. The programme was described as providing evidence
of American good faith.

Next came a statement that, earlier that day, the US had established a strong military cordon around Mecca. For the time
being, that cordon would not interfere with the free passage of
people into or out of Mecca. However, the US reserved the right
to close that cordon should it deem such action was required.
There followed an outline of the action the US would take in various circumstances. The statement stressed the word "would."
These actions would definitely be taken, not just considered.

Should there occur any incident of a terrorist nature, anywhere in the world, attributable to any Islamic group, the cordon around Mecca would be closed. People would be allowed to
leave Mecca but not enter.

A second incident would result in the immediate suspension
of the aid programme to Afghanistan. The emphasis was on the
word "immediate." Planes or trucks bound for Afghanistan would
be turned around. Food or goods inside the country, which had
not yet been distributed, would be removed from the country.

A third incident would see Mecca reduced to dust by artillery and cruise missiles with those in Mecca given twelve hours' notice.

Any further incident would result in even more dire consequences. The statement listed twenty cities with a predominantly Moslem population. Any incident beyond the third would see the name of one of these cities being drawn from a hat. Forty-eight hours' notice would be given before that city would be obliterated by nuclear missiles.

The statement concluded with a declaration that the gloves were off. For decades, the US and its allies had acted with restraint in the face of continued provocation and cowardly attacks on civilians. If the jihadists considered civilian populations to be fair game, the US was now going to adopt the same view of those Muslim populations on whose behalf the jihadists claimed to act. It did not wish to cause mass casualties but would have no compunction in causing extensive destruction.

The initial response from most of the world was one of outrage although some commentators took a differing view. "No incidents, no destruction. No incidents, an end to famine in Afghanistan," they pointed out. The world waited to see how the jihadists would respond and whether the US would go through with its threats. The wait was quite brief. Just two weeks later, an Islamic group claimed responsibility for a bomb attack in Turin. The cordon was closed. Some groups of pilgrims sought to break through the cordon but were forcibly repelled. Nineteen pilgrims died.

Three weeks later, Madrid suffered an attack by a suicide bomber who shouted, "Allah Aktar." The aid programme stopped.

As further weeks passed, many began to hope that no further attacks would occur. That hope was extinguished by an attack in Glasgow. Mecca was no more. This attracted outrage in Muslim countries, but much of that outrage was directed at the Jihadists. Ten days later, a joint statement was issued by several Islamic groups. This stated that Jihad had been suspended but that they reserved the right to reinstate it should the US commit any act against the Islamic faithful. This was as close to a total surrender as the US could expect.

For the next few years, the world was comparatively peaceful as this later version of "Pax Americana" prevailed. That situation was not to last as memories of the horrors of war faded, and both old and new disputes caused tensions to rise. War broke out in various theatres. India fought Pakistan. Iran attacked a number of gulf states. Brazil went to war with its northern neighbours.

During our European trips, I felt a little guilty at enjoying the sights in daylight hours when Besil was confined to the local base. However, she took full advantage of the nighttime economy. Unsurprisingly, proximity to Monte Carlo prompted a visit to the casino. Before we went, I shared some concerns with Besil. Her exploits in Vegas and bridge competitions in the US had not attracted much media attention outside the English-speaking world. This meant we could visit European towns and cities incognito. The only exception to this would be casinos, especially in Monte Carlo. There was a real risk that she would be recognised. By now, Lethal Linnet should look like a woman in late middle age, whereas Besil was still a very attractive thirty-something. Her backstory would have to be doctored.

My fears were realised when, during our time at a roulette table, a voice with a strong Texan accent boomed out behind us. "Howdy Lethal. Are you here to break the bank in Monte Carlo?" It was Texas Tom, one of the opponents at the final table when she had won the world championship. At that time, he had been one of the youngest participants. Now he was middle-aged. "Perchance, are you mistaking me for my mother?" replied Besil. "Doggone it, I think I must be. It was years ago that she kicked my butt. You could only have been a young child back then. But you sure take after your mom. She was a mighty fine-looking lady."

Tom then turned his attention to me. "I seem to remember you being at that final table as well. She kicked your butt early on. But hold on, it could not have been you. The guy I remember would be a resident in Boot Hill, by now." I told him his memory was not too bad. I had been told I resembled my paternal uncle with whom I shared my name. So far as I was aware, he was friendly with Lethal Linnet and had taken part in poker championships.

Tom said he was on his way to a high stakes poker table and suggested we join him. "So, you are looking for another scud at her?" I joked. "Not at all," he replied. "I am remembering how much I regretted being too shy back in the old days. I really fancied Lethal, although I guess I wasn't the only one. I might be too old for her daughter but, even if you aren't going to dine, there is no harm in looking at the menu." Knowing what Tom meant by high stakes, I purchased a large quantity of chips.

During the following couple of hours, Tom's derriere became reacquainted with Besil's feet as he lost over a quarter of a million euros. I did not fare that much better but managed to restrict my losses to less than 50,000 euros. Between them, the other four at the table contributed a further 450,000 euros to Besil's winnings. Yet, as she gathered her chips, she might as well have been playing for pennies or even matchsticks. She was expressionless.

She handed the chips to me to cash because, unlike Caesar's Palace, this casino was not going to hand out that amount of cash. The cashier simply credited the money electronically to my bank account. This was one occasion when Northern Ireland remaining in the single market proved useful. It might take a day or two for the money to reach my account but, that method of payment would not have been possible to anywhere else in the UK.

Back in Newry, the normal routine returned until the day I read that Sarah had passed away in her mid-nineties. She was my last link with the Newry I knew before my sojourn at Knocknashee. I dug out a dark suit and black tie and attended the funeral mass in Newry Cathedral. Afterwards, in St Mary's Cemetery, Esme came over to thank me for my presence and invite me to join the family and close friends for lunch in the Canal Court Hotel.

I shared a table with Esme and her husband, Peter; her daughter, Clara; Clara's fiancé, Jake; and Esme's elderly uncle, Jimmy. Esme introduced me to Clara as the customer Granny had talked about. Clara did the mental arithmetic and concluded that, if I had been older than Great Granny Janet, I must be over a hundred and twenty. At this, Jake's ears perked up. He was a reporter for the Newry Reporter with aspirations for greater things. As I prepared to leave, he asked if I would let him do a feature piece in the *Reporter*. I was not too keen on the idea but agreed he could come to the house two days later on the Wednesday morning. He explained that the paper went to press on the Tuesday night meaning that Tuesdays were always a bit manic.

His visit would necessitate switching off the time dilator, so I warned the Carnacans it would not be advisable to visit during that time. Apart from anything else, their presence would only prompt questions that I would find too difficult to answer. Besil was having nothing of that. She argued that our links were already well documented, and Jake was certain to ask about her. She would like to be there during the interview saying that, if I refused, she would come and knock at the door anyway. To avoid exposure to sunshine, she stayed over the night before, in a separate room I would add.

Jake had done his homework. Having googled my name, he knew about my participation in the world poker championships and my successes in American bridge competitions. From the latter, he had found the link between Lethal Linnet and me. He had even unearthed information on my participation in local bridge clubs, NIBU, CBAI, and IBU competitions, my chairmanship of NIBU and presidency of IBU. His first question was whether the man who became NIBU Chairman in 2009 was the same person to whom he was now talking in 2082. Photographs from my periods as Chairman and President show a man who looked to be in his late fifties would put that man somewhere around a hundred and thirty.

I had given considerable thought to what I was going to tell Jake. I concluded that telling the truth about my own age was the only possible way forward. Telling an American poker player that it was my uncle he had played against was one thing. But a journalist, however inexperienced, with the bit between his teeth was a different matter. He would have little difficulty in demonstrating the falsity of that fiction. Besil's situation was different. My longevity was surprising enough. For another person to be displaying a similar lack of the aging process would be just incredible, so I decided Besil would need to again play the role of Lethal's daughter.

I showed Jake my birth certificate and passport which, through Ixos's good offices, I had kept up to date at all times. I also supplied sundry details regarding my early life which he was able to check. Included was information regarding my grandmother's residence in The Red Row, a.k.a. O'Neill Avenue, her neighbours in the late 1950s and '60s, and a cousin's grocery business on John Mitchell Place. Also featured were my various successes in first aid competitions organised by the Order of Malta. These had been reported in the *Armagh Observer*. Jake was utterly convinced and really excited. Not only would the story be front page news in the *Reporter* but, with careful timing, taking the story to the national press and national television would be rewarding for him.

The next month was spent either giving or fending off interviews. A number of universities were keen to study my general health and genetic makeup. I soon realised why some people became intoxicated with fame. There was, however, one downside. Inevitably, the extensive media coverage brought the matter to the attention of the Civil Service Pension Scheme and the National Insurance Pension Scheme. Each sought some proof that I was genuinely a hundred and thirty years old and not some fraudulent imposter. By then, the state pension age had reached seventy, and I did not look old enough. After much thought, I came up with two possible sources of that proof, both of them something of a long shot. My first employment had been with the NI Blood Transfusion Service. As a staff member, my blood had been fully typed, and I dug out the old card showing not just that I was group O and Rhesus negative but my typing in all of the other systems including Lewis, Lutheran, Kidd, Kell, MN, P, and S. I was aware that, theoretically at least, somebody else might have an identical blood typing but the probability of that was vanishingly small. Even if the old NIBTS records, which would confirm the validity of my card, were unavailable, testing a blood sample would show that the blood typing on the card coincided with mine.

The other possible source was a record of my fingerprints. Around 1973, a girl with whom I had consensual sexual intercourse, lied about the event to her mother who was seeking an explanation for certain stains on her clothing. She had accused me of rape. I was interviewed under caution by the RUC, and my fingerprints were taken. Following that interview, during which I provided a frank account of events, I heard nothing further from the RUC. I was now hoping that the card with my prints had not alone survived but could be located. It would provide absolutely conclusive proof.

In the event, the fingerprints were located and accepted as irrefutable proof that I was who I said I was. I was not required to provide the blood sample. The media frenzy had abated somewhat but was still demanding of my time. Some requests, I was happy to meet. The Old Newry Society asked me to give a couple of talks about my memories of Newry from the 1950s onwards. Having enjoyed some of their talks when I first lived in Newry, I was happy to comply. The two talks I gave were very well attended, and each followed the same format. I spoke for around half an hour and then answered questions and entered into general discussion with the audience for a further hour or so. People were interested in my recollections of things, such as the metal swing bridge over the canal, seeing boats, like the Oak and Alder, sailing up the ship canal to the Albert Basin and how Water Street and North Street looked before the destruction wrought by the construction of a dual carriageway through road. But it was the simple things that fascinated them most. I recalled walking along Chapel Street in the late 1950s. The footpath consisted of concrete flags, most of which had acquired a dirty grey colour. But, before each front door was a semi-circular area of clean concrete. Housewives scrubbing their hallway also scrubbed the area of pavement within their reach. That practice gradually disappeared during the sixties.

Each evening concluded with light refreshments. On the second occasion, I was buttonholed by a lady who asked me if I remembered Ciaran Donnelly. Following a couple of moments reflection, I said, "Local historian." It emerged that I was talking to Ciaran's great grand-niece Sheila. Ciaran had bequeathed all of his papers to the museum in Bagenal's Castle with the stipulation that they be available to any member of the Old Newry Society. Following my first talk, Sheila had a vague recollection of having seen my name in some of those papers. It took a few hours trawling through the various items, which had never been properly catalogued, but finally she found Ciaran's notes on his and my research into Mickey McAteer. What had really intrigued her was the mystery surrounding Mickey's age. She wanted to know whether I had ever made any further progress and was disappointed when I told her I had not. She had carried out her own investigations a few years ago but had encountered the same difficulties as had Ciaran and me. She then worried me by saying that she found it fascinating that a man who later became truly ancient had once shown great interest in a man who also might have been ancient. I breathed a sigh of relief when she added, "Still, I suppose stranger things have happened." I quickly steered the conversation to other topics.

Very rarely did those seeking to interview me ask anything other than the same old questions. *Cosmopolitan* was an exception. The final question was one I had been expecting but this was the first time it was put to me. "Do you still have sex at one hundred and thirty?" I gave the ambiguous answer: "Desires do not magically disappear at retirement age." Above that paragraph appeared a photograph of me with Besil, who happened to be present during the interview. Otherwise, dealing with all the attention became a bit of a grind. So much so that I told Besil and Ixos, I needed to get away for a while.

It was Ixos who came up with the brilliant idea. He had listened to my stories of various bridge congresses. He would have liked to have attended one but, because each of the main competitions included a daylight session in a naturally lit room, this was im-possible. Could we organise one of our own? My first reaction was that it was a ridiculous idea until Ixos outlined his thinking as to the venue and participants. It was a brilliant idea.

Aware that the ordinary base would be far too small a venue, Ixos had thought of Antarctica. On its own, any spaceship would be too small, but the entire fleet parked on that landmass was interconnected. The ships were only feet apart, and tunnels of stuff ran from the left side door of one to the right side door of its neighbour. Each ship could accommodate a section of sixteen tables. Five ships would be sufficient for a congress involving one hundred and sixty pairs. Ixos communicated with the Antarctic base and produced a list of one hundred and fifty-eight pairs say-ing that left room for Besil, Citas, Jamil and him. I was the only person with any experience in tournament directing he observed.

The normal congress in Ireland takes place over a weekend with a single session of Mixed Pairs, two sessions of Congress Pairs and two of Congress Teams. Such would not be sufficient to satisfy Ixos. "Why not all play all?" he asked. He had a point. Spreading the congress over several days would not be a problem. If Ixos, Citas, and Besil were in any way representative in the speed at which they played, thirty-two boards could be played in a ses-sion lasting between two and a half and two and three-quarter hours. We could easily fit in three sessions per day. Ten sessions would be enough for all to play all. Thinking about how tight the competition was likely to be, with many flattish boards, it might need the full three hundred and twenty boards to separate competitors.

Similar considerations applied to a team competition. I thought that five sessions would be the minimum required. Thus, the congress would run for five days or almost eleven terrestrial months.

The more I thought about it, running this congress was going to be a mammoth undertaking. Firstly, the seventy-five sets of boards needed had to be sourced as did three hundred and twenty bidding boxes, 2,400 decks of cards and eighty bridge tables. Almost 5,000 personal score cards were also required. It made sense to purchase them directly from the manufacturers. So, I signed a three-year lease on premises in a nearby retail park and set up Carnac Bridge Supplies. To cover the possibility of some customers actually coming in and buying stuff, I bought in significantly more than I needed along with some bridge books and literature. To be on the safe side, I purchased two Duplimates® for dealing the boards.

The computer scoring system was problematic. The normal competition saw results from individual tables transmitted wirelessly to a server attached to a laptop or PC. In the stuff-clad environment of the spaceships, which were linked only by narrow corridors, I could foresee difficulties. A belt-and-braces approach seemed desirable. So, I acquired six laptops all loaded with ScorebridgeTM software; six servers would allow for one spare and one hundred Bridgemates, which allowed for the failure of some. At the end of each session, I would need to transfer the scores from each section's laptop to the sixth laptop, which would merge all five sections.

Dealing 2,400 boards is a lengthy operation even with two Duplimates®, so I was very grateful for the assistance provided by Magas and a couple of the other crew members.

Just when I was about to tell Ixos we were all set and ready to go, I realised I had overlooked one vital matter. So focussed had I been in acquiring all of the bridge equipment that I had overlooked seating. Most of the seating on the spaceships was in the nature of low couches and totally unsuitable for sitting at a card table. There were some suitable chairs but only a very few. Ordering and awaiting delivery of three hundred and twenty folding chairs would push us back by over a month. It also meant we would need two spaceships to transport the stuff to Antarctica.

I cursed myself for my own stupidity until I answered the door one morning to find a woman, aged somewhere in her fifties, standing on the doorstep. She introduced herself as Grainne Galbraith, which meant nothing to me until she added that her mother was Evelyn Simpson, whose maiden name had been O'Gallagher. The penny dropped. She was my great granddaughter! Without my stupidity, I would already have departed for the Antarctic, and we might never have met. I invited her inside and flicked off the time dilator behind my back as soon as I could. Even though I did it within a minute, I was acutely aware that around an hour of terrestrial time had elapsed. Fortunately, Grainne's visit lasted quite a while so that whenever we left the house to head into Newry, she was only mildly surprised when she noted the time.

When my wife and I separated, later to divorce, my three sons took their mother's side, and I had no communication from any of them since. I only discovered Evelyn's existence, and that of her brother, Myles, when a Google search showed announcements in the personal column of the *Daily Telegraph*. I sent each of them birthday cards, enclosing a small cash donation, but never received any acknowledgement. I had not sent any cards beyond their eighteenth birthdays.

Grainne informed me that she had been aware of me being her great grandfather as she was interested in genealogy. She knew that her mother had called to my house on a couple of occasions just after she finished university. Evelyn had been over to visit her grandmother in Newcastle and had taken the opportunity to call at my place in Newry. On each occasion, knocking on the door did not elicit any reply, and the front vertical blinds were closed. On the second occasion, she spoke to some of the neighbours. They told her that when I first lived there, they noticed me out and about most days. But, even before the first COVID lockdown, I had not been seen so much. In later years, my appearances had been very infrequent. So far as they knew, I had not moved out, but nobody could recall seeing me for several years before Evelyn's 2038 visit.

I felt guilty about lying to Grainne telling her that I had been travelling quite a bit in recent years. At least that bit was the truth though very far from the whole truth. I wondered what had prompted her visit at this time. Surely, she would have thought I was long since deceased. Grainne said that she had indeed thought that to be the case. But then there had been a media storm about this person named Tony O'Gallagher, who was a hundred and thirty years old. Her initial assumption had been that it was pure coincidence that this celebrity shared his name with her ancestor. She had retained this belief for the next few years until one evening when she had watched a quiz show. One question, which the contestant had failed to answer correctly, had been, "What is the full name of the world's oldest man?" when the correct answer had been revealed, it rang a bell. Anthony Colmcille Malachy Paschal O'Gallagher. She had checked her copy of the family tree and found the same full name. Now, coincidence had become a very, very remote possibility. Not many people had four forenames. None of the forenames were very common. The odds of two persons, not from the same family, sharing all five names were astronomical. The clincher was the date of birth. A little research revealed both had been born in London on 9 April 1952.

Grainne said that the discovery had been mind-blowing. My appearance was even more mind-blowing. If she did not know differently, she would put me in my sixties. Indeed, I could pass for late fifties. How had I managed to stay looking so young? Even more puzzling, she added, was that she had with her copies of photographs taken in 2012 and 2013. Back then, whilst I could have passed for early to mid-fifties, my appearance had been fairly normal for my age. It was almost as if my aging process had suddenly been frozen. We talked on this topic for a long time, with Grainne postulating a range of explanations with varying degrees of improbability but discarding each in turn.

Eventually, I was able to steer the conversation into other areas. Her grandfather, Ciaran, had enjoyed a very successful career with First Derivatives rising to a position just short of board level. Her granny, Maddy, had been able to abandon full-time employment as they were financially secure. Instead, she worked part-time running the business she and Ciaran had set up to exploit his photographic skills. Both had passed away within the last twelve years.

Her mother had followed her maternal grandfather and two paternal uncles into the medical profession. Just like those three, she attained the position of Consultant, in oncology, in her case. It was ironic that she was currently undergoing treatment for bone cancer. Although she was far from young, medical advances in recent years had resulted in more effective treatments than those previously available, and the prognosis was favourable. I expressed a wish to meet my granddaughter, and Grainne reckoned her mother would be delighted. She tried ringing her there and then but could not get through. I told her that mobile coverage was pretty poor where we were, which was technically true because the stuff wrapper around the house blocked the signal.

Grainne did get through to her mother whenever I took her out for a meal in the Italian restaurant on the mall. Evelyn and I could have talked all night but, as the starters arrived, I agreed to travel over to visit her. Grainne was travelling back by ferry to England the following day, but I did not want to spend a long time at normal-time speed travelling there, visiting Evelyn and travelling back by terrestrial means. So, I invented some business interests both in Armagh and near Birmingham. I would supposedly fly over after sorting out some stuff in Armagh. During my visit to Evelyn near Oxford, I would need to attend a couple of meetings near Birmingham. Of course, I had no such notion. I would either take the base vehicle on my own to the base near Oxford or ask Besil to come with me. I could make two or three visits to Evelyn each lasting a couple of hours and travel back after three terrestrial days. I would need to be in normal time for only a few hours.

Besil was very keen to take me. She had enjoyed the time we had spent there on our second trip to Britain. She suggested that I book a table in the Randolf, where we had eaten before. She most definitely had an appreciation for the finer things in life.

Evelyn looked quite frail but was in good spirits. As a child, she had asked who Grandad Tony was, but her father was very sparing with information. She had two other grandads because Maddy's parents had separated, and each had a new partner. But Grandad Tony always sent really good birthday cards, and she loved shaking them and watching the £20 note fall out. Her younger brother, Myles, did not really care what sort of card was sent as long as it contained a £20 note. Myles had emigrated some thirty years earlier and lived in Montevideo. She had emailed him after talking to me. Initially, he had been sceptical and suggested that I was some sort of con artist who was likely to try and defraud her. He only came round after Grainne sent him all of the relevant information and described the rather impressive interior of *Domhain Eile*. He had then suggested that Evelyn tell me I was over fifty years behind with the birthday cards.

Since discovering that I was still alive, Evelyn had done a lot of research and talked to some gerontologists she knew. All of them knew about me, and I was a source of much bafflement. There was a consensus among them that a man reaching one hundred and thirty years was not beyond the realms of possibility, although it had always been thought that women would continue to enjoy a greater life expectancy. But they would have expected a person of that age to show real signs of aging. Yet, what they had seen in photographs and during television appearances was a middle-aged man. Now, I was pushing towards one hundred and forty, an age which was considered unachievable. Apparently, some of them had nicknamed me Tortoise Tony because of the longevity of some of those creatures and the research underway in two laboratories.

I was aware that several laboratories were competing to be the first to unlock the secrets of my great age. Most were examining my DNA in painstaking detail. I had been happy to give them the relevant samples. I knew they were all barking up the wrong tree, but I wanted to appear cooperative. Two of them were comparing my DNA with that of fifty other people with the DNA from other long-lived species, such as giant tortoises. The idea was to try and identify a gene sequence common to the other species and me, which was not found in other humans. One researcher was on record as saying that, once the gene was identified, he hoped to genetically engineer long-lived humans.

I would have loved to tell my granddaughter the whole truth. By now, she was just about the last link with my life prior to discovering the Carnacan presence on Earth. But doing so could effectively ruin the humanity project. I really could not go down that road because I felt a real sense of obligation to the Carnacans. They had brought me into their world and have given me some remarkable experiences. Without them, I would have spent my remaining days in Newry living alone. Evelyn might agree to keep my secret, but it would not be fair to her to tell her such an amazing story and then ask her to keep it to herself. If she made the matter public, I would have betrayed my friends at Knocknashee and all of the other bases.

I concluded my third visit to Evelyn by agreeing to keep in contact with her and Grainne even though I knew this promise might prove difficult to keep. At most bases, I could go outside the barrier and phone or email them. Antarctica might be different because I suspected that there might not exist much coverage for either on that continent. But I did think it should be possible to use a satellite phone there, so I bought one of those devices.

On our return to Knocknashee, we still had a couple of weeks to wait before the chairs were delivered. I used the time to deliver a couple more bridge lessons to the those intending to play in the congress. Up to then, I had given the Carnacans limited information on bidding systems. Besil, because she had partnered me in high-level competition, was the only one aware of anything other than the standard Acol systems, which used either weak or strong no trump and four or five card majors. I now brought to their attention systems, such as Precision, Blue Club, and Polish Club. I suggested each partnership decide for themselves which to use.

Finally, our chairs arrived, and then the two spaceships arrived. In addition to the bridge stuff, we also loaded sets of books. Ixos informed me of the long-standing requests from several bases in the antipodes that I visit. It made sense to carry out those visits on our way back from Antarctica. During the flight, we had a very interesting conversation. I happened to mention a dream I had the night before. Besil volunteered that she had never dreamed before she arrived on Earth and that she only dreamed after consumption of alcoholic drink. Citas informed me he had experienced his first dream whilst convalescing following his encounter with the bull. Ixos confirmed that his dreaming also began on Earth and was also linked to consumption of alcohol. We communicated with Knocknashee and brought the medic into the conversation. Argil explained that, whilst dreaming was not unknown on Carnac, it was not commonplace. In all instances that had been studied, it was thought to have been occasioned by either injury or illness, especially fever. Carnacan scientists believed that dreaming was a manifestation of some bodily malfunction. Since the humanity project had commenced, they had become aware that most humans had frequent dreams. They would have liked to conduct a large-scale study to investigate whether it was an innate feature of humanity or whether external factors were involved. Unfortunately, the study was not possible without prejudicing the entire humanity project. The information regarding a possible link with alcohol consumption was interesting and would be communicated to Carnac.

If one asked any Tournament Director whether he would like to singlehandedly direct a bridge congress with one hundred and sixty pairs participating, the short answer would be "No!" For any competition involving that number of pairs, there would be a team of TDs in place, consisting of the principal director and three or four assistants. It was desirable that any request for a TD ruling on any alleged infraction be dealt with promptly. This required a TD in each playing area, if more than one was being used, or in each part of a large playing area. In practice, one TD for each section would be the norm. Many would have questioned my sanity. What they did not know was that I did not foresee any infractions at all.

That indeed proved to be the case. There was not a single request for a ruling throughout the entire congress. Much as I expected, competition was extremely tight. At the conclusion of the first session, there was a four-way tie for the lead on 50.95%. Contrast that with the typical leading score in a human competition of around 65%. As the sessions went by, the gaps gradually widened but, even after nine sessions with Mitchel movements, any one of several pairs still held hopes of winning out during the concluding Howell. The final winning score was 52.97%, which was just 0.06% in front of the runners-up, who were Besil and Ixos. Jamil and Citas finished a creditable ninth. Naturally enough, these two pairs played together in the teams which they won.

The visits in Australia and New Zealand proved enjoyable. I took the opportunity to try and track down my Aussie cousins. My father had two sisters, one of whom joined a convent and was part of a group who had moved to Perth in Western Australia in 1933. Subsequently, she left the convent, married, had a daughter and became a violent alcoholic. I remember, as a child aged ten, hearing of plans for this cousin to come to live with us in Armagh. The situation must have been bad for anyone to contemplate sending a seven-year-old girl halfway round the world to live with people who, though blood relatives, were strangers. The plan was not carried out. Because back then, disgraced nuns were not considered suitable subjects in polite conversation, I heard nothing more about either aunt or cousin. The other sister never married and died intestate in 2008. The estate consisted of a very large bank balance. Since no property was involved, I took on the administration of the estate. It would have been pretty straightforward had it not been for the need to track down this cousin who was potentially entitled to half the estate. Initial research brought me copies of the aunt's birth, marriage and death certificates and the cousin's birth certificate. But what next? Should I advertise in local, regional, and national newspapers?

The abandoned plan to have the cousin fostered by my parents left the possibility that she had been adopted in Australia. Had that been the case, Cousin Maureen would have no entitlement. By chance, I found the website for the Past Adoption Agency in Western Australia. I contacted them, and they agreed to check the old records. When one of their employees informed me that there was no record of any adoption, she added that the case had intrigued her, and she had done some research. This had revealed that Maureen had married and bore two children. These children were on the electoral role, but Maureen was not. I asked that she write to the children giving them my contact details and informing them that I was seeking to contact their mother regarding an inheritance. In the absence of any reply from the children, this employee did a bit more digging and spoke to Maureen's husband to discover that Maureen was teaching English in Hong Kong. She and I exchanged emails, photographs, etc. for two weeks before I had to remind her that I needed to send her a significant chunk of money. Maureen was less excited about the money than having found out that she had five full cousins.

I had met Maureen just once and shown her around Newry just as I had shown her daughter Janelle around Newry when she made the trip to Ireland a couple of years previously. It was most probable that Janelle and her brother were deceased, but they may have had children. I was disappointed to discover that neither Janelle nor her brother, Matt, had ever had any children. That branch of the family had come to an end.

Back home, life settled back into some sort of routine. It would have been easy to become something of a recluse because people seemed to think that a celebrity like me was public property. It was rare that I could visit the supermarket, Off License, pub, restaurant, or any other venue without total strangers approaching me either wanting to talk or seeking selfies with me. Even staying in *Domhain Eile* was not without its problems. Regularly, people turned up on the doorstep. Many of them seemed to think they had some sort of entitlement to be invited in for a chat. On average, I received over one hundred letters a week from all parts of the globe. Some were addressed to Tony O'Gallagher, Ireland. A few even found their way to The Really Old Man in Ireland. Thankfully, my email address had never been published. Even so, a few emails got through to my inbox. It was likely they had tried various possibilities, including tonyogallagher@******. I ignored these, not even deleting them, because once one such correspondent had confirmation, they had the right email address it could have entered the public domain.

In spite of the high volume, I was conscientious in opening all my mail and at least skim-reading it. A large percentage of it was quickly despatched to the shredder. Some requests I was happy to meet. Several schools asked me to address their A-level students and take part in question-and-answer sessions. I gained the impression that teenagers regarded my extreme longevity rather differently than their parent's generation. The young people viewed anyone over, say seventy, as a crumbly. My hundred and sixty years plus were not radically different from another's eighty-five years. It was of degree.

I was truly delighted when one school asked me to be guest speaker at its prize night. My sons had each attended St Louis Grammar School in Kilkeel. When my youngest son, Kevin, was in upper sixth, my wife and I decided to give something to the school in recognition of the excellent education our sons had received. The school had prizes for some but not all subjects. We decided to donate the O'Gallagher Chemistry Prize. In those days, there was a cut-glass factory known as Tyrone Crystal, and I commissioned a piece from them. It took the form of a conical flask and a beaker holding a spatula mounted on a wooden base. The school were so worried about potential damage to the piece that, although it was presented to the prize winner on that night, it was not permitted to leave the school premises.

On arrival at the school, I found that the prize was still intact. The Principal presented me with a list of the names of every recipient annotated with biographical details for many of them. It was amazing to learn that one recipient of the O'Gallagher Prize had, some thirty years later, become a Nobel Laureate. I also learned that I was the only person to perform as guest speaker some seventy-five years after his son was similarly honoured.

Michael, who achieved consultant status at a young age, had addressed the gathering in 2037. I began my speech by stating that the only previous occasion on which I had spoken from the same stage had been one hundred and forty-three years previously when I had led my school-debating team when it was drawn to meet St Louis in a competition sponsored by Aer Lingus.

I was always happy to give my support to fundraising events for charities. On one occasion, the charity was able to sell two hundred signed photographs of me at £80 each. On another night, the charity auctioned a poem I had composed. As it was wintertime, Besil was able to accompany me to the event in Belfast. Somehow, I think many assumed that the poem was about her. The lyrics were as follows:

My Soul It Sings

My soul it sings with unbridled joy
A duet with the golden sun
Who shines upon my own true love
Warming her womanly form.

My soul it sings with unbridled joy
A duet with the silver moon
Who watches over my own true love
Lighting her dreams of me.

My soul it sings with unbridled joy
A duet with the gentle breeze
Who drifts around my own true love
Bringing her scent to me.

My soul it sings with unbridled joy
A duet with mine own heart
For I have found my own true love
From her, I ne'er will part.

I had printed the poem on top quality paper, signed it and had it framed. I had hoped it might realise a few hundred pounds for the charity. I stood in amazement as I listened to the auctioneer begin: "I have commission bids of fifteen, eighteen, twenty, twenty-two, twenty-five, 28,000. Will anyone give me 30,000?" A flurry of bidding followed with the hammer finally falling at £67,500. What a result! The buyer might have been less delighted with his purchase had he known that the poem was originally written by me in 2017.

I had often wondered why a painting, of no great merit, could achieve a high price just because the artist was famous in some other field. Now I witnessed that phenomenon first hand. The poem is not bad but by no means could it be regarded a great piece of poetry.

Besil and I continued to undertake short trips away. Occasionally, we went to the continent, but her favourite destination was London. To be more precise, Le Gavroche restaurant. My celebrity status ensured that we were always able to secure a table even at short notice. Over time, we became accustomed to the stares we attracted on entering that establishment and to being the subject of photographs taken clandestinely on mobile phones. The sommelier took to greeting me, "Well, young man, to which great wine will you treat the lady tonight?"

One January evening, we had a most unusual interruption during our meal. We had just finished our starters when a waiter came to the table. He informed me that a lady was seeking to have a brief conversation with me. He added sotto voce, "It is the Prime Minister." I acceded to the request to discover that the PM wanted my autograph. Not for herself, but for her twelve-year-old nephew, Joshua. He was almost obsessed with me and maintained a scrapbook devoted to me. His birthday was the following day. The PM produced a birthday card she had purchased and asked me to sign it instead of her. She could get another one.

I was happy to inscribe, "Happy birthday, Joshua. I hope you live for even longer than me." Next, she asked a waiter to take a photograph of Besil, her, and me.

As she walked back to her own table, she turned and came back over. She informed us that she was hosting Joshua's birthday party the following evening in number ten. Were we able to attend, it would be the most marvellous surprise for him. So it was that the following evening saw me enjoying a meal accompanied by some rather good Chateau Margaux. Besil surprised me by remarking to the PM, "I never thought I would be attending a drinks party in Downing Street." I added, "Just as well we are not in lockdown." The PM gave a puzzled glance before saying, "Of course. You were alive in Bojo's day."

Joshua was remarkably well informed about me. His scrapbook covered most aspects of my life apart from my contact with the Carnacans. He quizzed me about this and that until he came to my participation in the world poker championship. He knew how to play the game and asked if Besil and I would join him at the card table. The PM and his father also played. It was the first occasion I ever played with Smarties as chips, each starting with a full packet and the various colours allocated different values. I had never seen Besil play so badly. The game concluded with Joshua wiping out his aunt and me with the same hand. His delight was obvious.

As we were leaving number ten, the PM thanked us for coming. She added that she suspected we might play slightly differently in a high stakes game. She had noted and appreciated our willingness to help put the finishing touch to a memorable evening for her nephew.

On returning from one such trip to London, I set to the task of dealing with the mountain of post that awaited me. A letter bearing an Armagh postmark was a real blast from the past. It was from Stephen Campbell. He was a great, great grandson of

Jim Campbell. The letter outlined how, when he first read Jake Jackson's articles about me, he had recognised my name. Jim and I had both dabbled in poetry during the early 1970s, and Jim had included four of my efforts in a booklet of his own poetry. We had lost contact when I moved to Belfast, but Jim continued to write poetry, and his son followed in his footsteps. Stephen had inherited his ancestor's papers. When Jake wrote about me, it was obvious to him that I was the other poet in his ancestor's booklet. For years, he had regarded this as just one of life's curiosities. But recently, whilst sitting in his dentist's waiting room, he was flipping through an old magazine and came across a report of the charity auction of my poem. Suddenly, that old booklet acquired a whole new significance. If one of my poems had fetched £67,000, what would four of them be worth? Was I willing to authenticate the booklet?

Not only did I remember that booklet, but I still had a copy of it. Two of my efforts were really quite poor, but the other two were reasonable. One was my first attempt at a love poem written before I became an atheist.

Nisitory

Words may praise the flowers so fair
Songs can sing of the sea so blue
But my pen may never ever
Show my love so true for you.

If I could fathom God's creation
Or plumb his deep eternal time
Describe the beauty of a snowdrop
Or the scent of mountain thyme.
If I could read that mind almighty
Which treasures you and treasures me,
Then I would write in words of wisdom
Of you, and me, and eternity.

The other was the only poem I had ever written that touched on the troubles.

A Nation's Dream

A dream in shreds through present deeds
Of endless greed and hate
By those who hold no higher thoughts
Who lust one cannot sate
Who feed on love and innocence
Warping heart and soul
Leading youth the left-hand path
To their satanic goal
Oh! land which kept the flame of faith
In days of pagan shame
Where are your saints and scholars now
Who brought you once such fame?
I pray they will return again
To this most troubled place
And aid us to our nation's dream
Of peace, and love, and grace.

I was happy to meet Stephen and did so in the Canal Court Hotel a few days later. He stated he was torn between putting the booklet up for auction and hanging on to a piece of family history. Certainly, he could do with the money, and he knew he could copy the poems, but parting with the only copy of the booklet would be a real wrench. I made his day by handing him my copy of the booklet, which I had already signed. A few weeks later, Ross's was packed with four telephone bidders and several online. Bidding commenced at £170,000 and reached £235,000. Even after commission, Stephen cleared £200,000. Had anyone ever suggested such an outcome to Jim and me back in the 1970s, we would have been flattered but still would have sent for the men in white coats.

Even with all the unwanted attention, life was good. Indeed, at times, I thought it was too good to last. My fears were realised one evening when Ixos called into *Domhain Eile*. "You might want to pour yourself a stiff drink," was his greeting. After I did so, he said, "We are leaving Earth."

Chapter 10

This was unexpected. The crew's tour of duty was not due to finish for many terrestrial years yet. My first thoughts were that World War Three was the reason for this decision, but Ixos assured me this was not the case. Certainly, that conflict was regarded with horror on Carnac, but nothing had occurred during the conflict which had not previously happened. "Then why?" was my question. If the worst conflict ever was not responsible, I could not imagine any other event or discovery which would have prompted this sudden termination of the humanity project.

When Ixos supplied me the full details behind the decision, much of the previously inexplicable suddenly made sense. The story began with the Carnacan space exploration programme. Without prejudging the outcome of the humanity project or the two similar projects on other planets, Carnac continued its search for other potential breeding partners. One of their spaceships had visited a planet that showed clear signs of having once hosted an advanced civilisation. They found the remains of large cities and what would have been technologically advanced infrastructure. But there was no sign of life on the planet. The reason became apparent when they found an enormous crater. It appeared that the planet had been impacted by a very large asteroid. The impact had wiped out all life.

Whilst exploring the planet, they noted a regular electromagnetic signal that appeared to originate from the next planet out from the star. On a trip to that planet, they followed the signal to its source, which looked as though it had been a small base of some sort. It was the only place on that super-chilled planet that had ever hosted any life. The Carnacans removed what seemed to have been electronic equipment and also several books and ledgers. These they brought back to the home planet for analysis by scientists.

That analysis was difficult in the extreme. There occurred much trial and error before they were able to operate the electronic equipment. And that was just the first step. The language used in the written and electronic records was totally alien to them. Deciphering it was not going to be an easy task. Without my realising it, my work with the linguists had been of some assistance to this task. It had given the linguists back on Carnac avenues to explore and eventually they began to translate the various records.

The first pieces translated described life on planet Kastus around 20,000 years ago. There existed a stable, orderly society with a population around 300 million. As on Carnac, all spoke the same language. Aggression was almost unknown with any instances linked to head injury or brain tumour. Life expectancy, at one hundred and seventy, was slightly greater than on Carnac. Societal organisation differed from Carnac. The first twenty-five years were devoted to learning, as was the case on Carnac but thereafter, a different pattern emerged. On Carnac, the next twenty-five years were spent in public service. On Kastus, that period could extend to around one hundred and twenty-five years, but the public service was not full-time. Part-time working was widespread. Some put in around half of what would be full-time hours whilst others just worked for as little as an average of one day in five. As long as they did the equivalent of twenty-five years of full-time service, they fulfilled society's expectation.

Scientific development was more advanced than that on Carnac in the same era. Part of this could be explained by the devastation wrought on Carnac by the pandemic 20,000 years earlier. The Kastusians did engage in some space travel but confined their journeys to their own solar system. Like the Carnacans, they had set up a base on the next planet out to avail of the

thinner atmosphere and the absence of electromagnetic interference. But they thought that voyages beyond their own system would constitute a waste of resources. Their fleet consisted of just three spaceships with none being capable of speeds
greater than five per cent of light speed.

Advanced as their technology was, they did not yet have part-par-
ticle, part-energy stuff nor the time dilator. Their scientists had
developed the basic technology for the latter but were encounter-
ing the same problem that beset the early efforts on Carnac. One
will never know whether, given sufficient time, the Kastusians
would have developed stuff and thereby a workable time dilator because they suffered their own disaster.

Their astronomers at the base on Planet Maxtus detected a
large rocky object that appeared to be on a collision course with
them. Their calculations indicated that impact would occur less
than five months later. Their estimates of the size of the object
and the force of the impact painted a grim picture. All life on
Kastus would be wiped out. Difficult decisions had to be taken
and taken quickly. Their production facilities for spaceships was
very limited. The first thought had been to investigate whether
the asteroid could be deflected away from Kastus. Their scientists knew that any such deflection would need to be sizeable.
The asteroid was not going to deliver a glancing blow nor even
hit the planet off-centre. Instead, the impact would be pretty much dead centre. An added complication was the direction
from which the asteroid was approaching. It was coming from
the far side of their sun, which meant that the planet and asteroid would approach the impact point from opposite directions
thereby giving the maximum possible impact speed. Could they
use an explosion of some sort to achieve the required deflection? They were aware of the explosive qualities of some chemical compounds, but preliminary computations showed they
would need an explosion of around ten parcal of energy (Ixos explained this was equivalent to approximately ninety megatons)

to take place immediately adjacent to the asteroid within the next three months. It would not be possible to transport such a massive quantity of explosive material into space.

The scientists were also aware of the theoretical possibility of creating an explosion of the required magnitude using nuclear fission or nuclear fusion. But that knowledge was purely theoretical. No such explosion had ever been created on Kastus, and the required technology would require to be developed from scratch. There wasn't even any existing design for such an explosive device. Any such project would require both the device and production technology to be designed and manufactured ab initio, the requisite fissile material to be sourced and refined and a space craft to be built to transport the device. The journey to the explosion point would require between three and four weeks so the time frame was reduced to two months. It just could not be completed in time.

That left evacuating the planet as the only option, and the absence of a large fleet of spaceships meant only a small-scale evacuation would be possible during the time available. The key decision came down to choosing between constructing around fifty spaceships each capable of carrying six people or two, possibly three, super spaceships with a capacity of 1,000 each. These were still in the concept stage, but the engineers were confident they could be built and would work. They reckoned two could certainly be built in time but were uncertain about the third. The decision was taken to build the super spaceships.

Work continued round the clock on their construction. Normally, such a project would have taken a couple of years, but decisions were made based on preliminary results from research and development experiments. The usual quality control checks were concertinaed but, even so, only two ships were completed in time.

The question of who would travel on these spaceships had been decided at an early stage. There existed a widespread consensus that the fairest method of selection was a random draw. Each person was allocated a ten-digit personal identification number. A computer programme was written to enable the selection to be truly random. Great care was taken to ensure the absence of any bias with the programme being independently audited by three groups of experts. Just about all activity, with the exception of spaceship construction, came to a halt during the draw. The first thousand would travel on the first ship to be finished, the next thousand on the second. The third thousand hoped that the third ship would be available.

I was puzzled by the decision to use random selection. Clearly, the intention was that the evacuees would eventually establish a new Kastusian population on some other planet. Would it not be desirable that all of the evacuees be of reproductive age? One would have thought that only those below a certain age should have been in the draw. "Not at all," Ixos informed me. The records revealed that, possibly uniquely, Kastusians retained the ability to reproduce throughout their entire lifetime. Their language had no word for menopause.

I also wondered about the reactions of the thousands of millions who were not selected. Was there not disaffection and unrest? "Why would there have been?" replied Ixos. "These people knew that the survival of the species was dependent on the success of the evacuation. Anything other than their full acquiescence could jeopardise that success. All would die at some time in the future. The impact from the asteroid would just bring that date forward. The priority was the survival of the species." He added that the Kastusians presumably had their own version of "Clanwe yashpak."

The final question to be decided concerned the route the spaceships would travel. Kastusian astronomers had little useful knowledge regarding the planets that might provide a future home. All they could provide was the location of planets that orbited a star of the right type at the right distance. This should mean that the climate, especially temperature, would be suitable. But they had no information on important matters, such as the composition of the atmosphere, pH of any seas and oceans, or the existence or otherwise of species who might prove to be predators.

A dilemma existed. Genetic considerations meant it was desirable that the evacuees travel together. A population of 2,000 was in itself small enough to give rise to concerns regarding inbreeding. Cut that to 1,000, and those concerns increased. But the spaceships could only travel a finite distance, and there was no guarantee that any of the first planets visited would be suitable. The chances of finding a suitable planet would be doubled if the two ships followed different routes. The solution was surprisingly simple. Astronomers plotted two courses that were more or less parallel to each other. This meant that if either group found a suitable new home, it could notify the other group, which would then rejoin them there.

Each group would report regularly to the base on Maxtus so that the information on Kastus could be updated for as long as possible. There was no guarantee that either group of evacuees would survive, and Kastus did not wish their society to disappear, leaving no trace of its achievements. If nothing else, they wanted others to be able to benefit from their technology should they be able to interpret the written and electronic records. The crew on the base were replaced with a group of twenty-five-year-olds. Thus, the base should be manned for a further century and a half. The electronic recording devices would continue to record indefinitely unless some malfunction occurred.

Departure day approached, and two days beforehand, a crowd began to assemble near the space centre, all seeking the best spot from which to observe the departure of the spaceships. The centre was surrounded by a vast empty plain, and, by the time the spaceships departed, the crowd stretched as far as the eye could see. Various estimates were published as to the size of that crowd. The consensus was that somewhere around one hundred and ten million people has been present. Almost all of the rest of the planet's population watched on television.

The previous evening, a television programme had been broadcast. It had a simple format. There were no speeches by administrative officials. Instead, a banner appeared at the bottom of the screen that read: "The future of Kastus." One by one, in numerical order, an announcer read the names of the 2,000 evacuees. These now included the first three people originally drawn for the third spaceship had it been ready in time. One was replacing a person who had died since the draw was made. The others took places vacated by two persons who had decided they would prefer to die on their home planet. As each name was read out loud, a photograph of that person appeared on the screen. The process was not rushed. Each image stayed on screen for five seconds, which meant the programme lasted for almost three hours. Most watched it in its entirety.

The spaceships left three days before the asteroid struck. Strangely, during the interim period, life seemed to return to almost normal. Whereas first the draw and later the departure had brought the planet to a standstill, the impending extinction did not have the same effect. On the morning of the expected impact many people showered, shaved, dressed and went off to school or work as if it were a normal day. Why this happened was discussed for many years by those at the base on Maxtus and the evacuees. At first glance, it made no sense. What was the point of starting some task that one knew for certain one would never complete? The medics on the spaceships suggested it was possibly the most effective coping mechanism. The asteroid impact with its fatal consequences could not be prevented, so just ignore it.

The astronomers on Maxtus watched the asteroid pass within 80,000 miles of their base and, a few hours later, smash into one of the continents on Kastus. Even from a distance of twenty-five million miles, it was clearly visible though their telescopes. They wondered if they were the only persons to have witnessed such an event.

As I listened to Ixos, I reflected on how, in one respect at least, humanity had been very fortunate. Carnac had suffered the most horrendous pandemic. Civilisation on Kastus had been obliterated by an asteroid, an event the probability of which was very small. By contrast, humanity had benefitted from a similar event. Had Earth not experienced its own asteroid impact, it was quite possible that dinosaurs or their evolutional descendants would still be the alpha species on the planet.

As had been feared by Kastusian scientists, the search for a new home planet would take time. Spaceship A reached its first target planet after almost seven years. Its stay was of a short duration. Sampling of the atmosphere showed that it was toxic. It contained almost two per cent sulphur dioxide, which also resulted in acidic seas and oceans.

A further eight years brought them to the second target. Here, the atmosphere was suitable even though it contained, at thirty two per cent, a larger concentration of oxygen than might have been expected. Using a precautionary approach, they orbited the planet at successively lower levels. Slowly, they realised that an unusual situation prevailed on the planet's surface. Even using their strongest telescopes and binoculars, they could not see any animal life. This was most unexpected. When they finally launched a small vessel, which carried a crew of four and was intended to land on the surface, they discovered the reason for this anomaly. The lower this craft descended, the higher the readings on their paxor (a type of Geiger counter). So high did those readings become that they aborted the mission, and the craft returned to the mother ship. The exercise was repeated at four other locations, which were spaced well apart.

On each occasion, the outcome was the same. The only occasion on which the paxor readings stayed within tolerable limits was when the craft hovered low over the centre of the largest ocean. They concluded that the planet's crust contained an unusually high concentration of some radioactive element, and the products of its decay could also be radioactive. Exactly which element was there could only be ascertained by analysis of samples. Obtaining these would not only be very dangerous but pointless. Nobody could survive on that planet.

Ten years later, the third target also possessed a poisonous atmosphere. This time, there was a significant concentration of ammonia. Nor had Spaceship B enjoyed any greater success. They had reached just two of their target list. One had too much sulphur dioxide in its atmosphere. The composition of the other planet's atmosphere would have been fine had there been enough of it. For whatever reason, the atmosphere at sea level was similar to what one would expect at a height of 40,000 feet. It could not sustain life.

En route to its fourth target, Spaceship A received a disturbing message from the other ship. Its navigation system was malfunctional, and repair was not possible. Its route through space was now dictated by its heading before the malfunction and the gravitational effects of the star field through which it was travelling. In time, it was likely to become a satellite of some star. It might continue to orbit that star until its supplies ran out. A preferable fate would be to follow a spiral orbit that terminated in vaporisation as the ship headed into the star's clutches. The latter proved to be the case.

Now the last hope of Kastus, Spaceship A reached its fourth target, a planet we now know to have been Earth. As the Kastusians carried out their analyses and observations, it appeared that this planet had real possibilities. The atmosphere was good. The climate was suitable. Background radioactivity was at a very low level. The was a varied flora and fauna. The clinching factor was the presence of a species who appeared remarkably similar to Kastusians. Was it possible that this species could provide reproductive partners and permit an expansion of the genetic pool?

They decided to observe this species for an extended period. The ship still contained supplies sufficient for many years so there was no urgency to make contact with this species. This observation could not be carried out from orbit, so they landed the spaceship. Not wanting to attract attention, they chose the summit of a mountain from where they could mount expeditions using the three small vessels carried by the ship.

Their initial thinking was very positive. The natives were, on average, a few inches shorter than the six foot two of their visitors with the females appearing to be a couple of inches shorter than the males. They were mostly of good physique. Most importantly, all seemed to be calm, even tempered and of good disposition. They appeared to have a well ordered society with groups cooperating in ventures to their mutual benefit. Parents took good care of their offspring who, like their Kastusian counterparts, were vulnerable during their first few years of life. Life expectancy seemed to be a lot lower than on Kastus. It was difficult to be certain, but few appeared to live much beyond thirty years. Aggression between natives was unknown, although they killed other species without compunction for food. All spoke the same language, of which the visitors had gained a rudimentary understanding. This language had quite a limited vocabulary.

Technologically, they were very backward. In some regions on the planet, the people were still essentially hunter-gatherers, although most people had transitioned to an agricultural existence. They kept small herds of animals, which supplied them with meat and milk. Other larger animals were used to pull implements employed to break up the soil before seeds were sown. These implements were fashioned from wood. Metal working was in its infancy. Iron was yet to be extracted from haematite, but items were being produced in bronze in some regions. Throughout the planet, items of varied sophistication were produced from clay baked in rudimentary ovens. Perhaps their most important achievement was their widespread use of the wheel.

Medical knowledge was extremely limited but interesting nonetheless. Various plants were widely used to treat fever, infection, and diarrhoea. The Kastusians observed with puzzlement the natives chewing the bark of a certain tree to relieve pain. Analysis in the laboratory on the ship revealed it contained a chemical featuring the salicylate compound. They wondered how the natives had discovered this analgesic.

Having spent thirty-four years travelling, the Kastusians could not study the native race for as long as they would have liked. The spaceship was full to capacity, so reproduction had been prohibited during their journey except to replace any who died en route. When a death occurred, a name was drawn at random. That person could seek a reproductive partner and create a new life. Almost two hundred of the original party had died. This restriction on reproduction continued even after landing on this planet as it had not yet been decided whether it was their final destination.

Three years after landing, the Kastusians assembled to debate the future course of action. Two decisions were required. All those aged fourteen or older had a vote giving an electorate of nine hundred and seven. The first vote was unanimous. They would stay on this planet. When the second question was put to the vote, eight hundred and sixty-seven voted in favour of making contact with the native species and interbreeding with them. Those who dissented would not be compelled to take a native breeding partner. They had a choice of whether to live in one of the proposed settlements on the planet or to remain on the spaceship. If they stayed on the ship, they could reproduce with their fellow dissenters. In time, their children could choose which course to follow. Those under fourteen years old would remain with their mother until old enough to make their own choice.

The intention was to create settlements, each containing around thirty people in places where the native population gave their agreement to the settlement and indicated a willingness to interbreed. At each proposed site, the spaceship landed nearby and a group of four went in one of the small craft to the nearest native settlement to seek agreement. Nowhere was there any problem. The native population were already aware of the Kastusian presence on the planet. They regarded the visitors with awe and were willing to cooperate with them. So willing were they that they frequently assisted in constructing dwellings for the Kastusians. The spaceship remained close by until the dwellings were ready. Supplies sufficient to feed the settlement until they harvested their first crops were left.

Throughout the voyage, the evacuees had made regular reports to the base on Maxtus. It was felt that it was important that a record be left of the history and achievements of Kastus. The base had been crewed by twelve twenty-five-year-olds when they left Kastus. It was hoped that reproduction between some of the crew one hundred and thirty years later would ensure that the base was crewed for around three hundred years. Communications could still be recorded by equipment at the base after that until the equipment malfunctioned. The only device capable of communicating with Maxtus was on the spaceship. Each of the three small craft could communicate with the ship so a system was devised whereby one of these craft would visit each settlement once every ten years to enable that settlement to make a report to the spaceship. The reports from the bases would be collated and a summary sent to Maxtus.

Two of those who chose to remain on the ship were Kaptan and Leptis. Each had been a small child when they left Kastus and were now in their thirties. They undertook the job of collating the settlement reports and making the reports to Maxtus. One hundred years later, they had a female child together whom they named Jeflis. Together, these three deserve credit for the information now available to us regarding events on Earth during the period following the Kastusian landing.

The first batch of reports were universally positive and optimistic. Kastusians had been made very welcome by the native population. Interbreeding was going well, with the Kastusians complying with the local practice of a couple staying together once they produced a child. Almost all of these couples had produced at least two children with over two-thirds having three and a fifth having four or five. As was the case with their purebred offspring, the native people, whether male or female, were attentive parents to crossbred children.

The Katusians had become the process of developing the native technology. In an effort to improve their living quarters, the first advance was the production of bricks for building dwellings. Prior to the Katusian arrival, these had consisted of interwoven branches, which supported a skin of dried mud. Even when the inside of the walls was hung with furs and animal skins, they were cold and draughty in the winter months. The natives already had experience of baking clay to produce pottery. It was simply a matter of showing them that the addition of vegetable matter, such as straw increased the strength of the product dramatically. Towards the end of the first decade, the first steps were taken in the process, which would lead to showing the natives how to produce iron. One of the scientists at one settlement began an exploration of the surrounding region collecting many rock samples. These, he wished to have analysed on the spaceship, but this would have to wait until the craft arrived to enable the settlement report to be made. Since only one scientist was left among those on board, the analysis would take much longer than usual. So, the results did not reach him by craft until six years into the second decade.

There was just the occasional note of slight concern in these first reports. A few settlements passed comments on about the crossbred children. Some, though not all, displayed hints of possessing undesirable traits such as a degree of selfishness and irritability. None of the authors of those comments thought it a matter of serious concern.

The second batch of reports outlined further progress on the technological front. The production of iron had commenced at two settlements. The quantities involved were quite small, but the native population were pleased at the uses to which they were put. Iron ploughs were much easier to use and more effective than the wooden version they replaced. Iron bands covering the circumference of wooden wheels eliminated the wearing away of the surface of wheels necessitating regular replacement. Perhaps the most significant use was to create iron tools, which could be used in quarrying stone to be used in construction.

All settlements were now reporting signs of undesirable traits in crossbred children, which were persisting into adulthood. Curiously, crossbreeds seemed to possess a remarkable ability to attract sexual partners whether crossbred, pure Kastusian or pure native. Only a very small number of children had been born to a crossbred parent, and all these were still in the infant stage. However, early indications were that the undesirable traits were more evident in this second generation.

Over the next few decades, the full extent of the problem became apparent. Purebreds had thought that the second generation of crossbreds had some undesirable, indeed nasty, traits, but the third generation was even worse. Selfishness and disregard for the well-being of others was bad enough. A propensity to use aggressive behaviour and physical violence was even worse especially when, on occasion, the violence appeared to be pre-planned. Nor was the aggression and violence just a matter of individuals behaving badly. Increasingly, crossbreds were acting in groups attacking other individuals or groups. On occasion, seizure of property, food, or other goods appeared to be the motive. On other occasions, it looked like violence for the sake of violence.

The crossbreds enjoyed one advantage when attacking purebred people. The purebreds lacked the aggression and propensity to violence, which would have been required if they were to fight back effectively. They were easy prey. An added advantage, when compared to humans, was a crossbred life expectancy that was ninety years for the first generation and, though it declined with each generation, was still around sixty years for the tenth generation. The enhanced ability to attract sexual partners remained and, to the few Kastusians left who survived, it became apparent that crossbreds would in time replace the native population.

Curiously, the crossbreds also exhibited some more attractive traits. They formed very close attachments to one another and seemed deeply affected when the other person in such an attachment died. Often, they moved their lips in a certain way revealing their teeth thus looking much better than normal. At times, they opened their mouths, threw back their heads and produced raucous noises.

Why the crossbreds were so different was the subject of much discussion and speculation amongst those few left on the spaceship. So concerned were they that they contacted the remaining Kastusians, suggesting that it might be best if they all departed this planet. But nobody relished the prospect of further years of space travel with no guarantee of finding another suitable planet. They decided to remain and report developments to Maxtus for as long as possible. They did not know whether any other species would ever read their reports, but they felt they owed a duty to the rest of the universe to leave as complete a record as possible.

One scientist, Prancan, postulated that the root cause of the problem might lie with allotropic molecules. He recalled a colleague being involved in research into that topic. He could not remember what the outcome had been, so a request was sent to Maxtus. The base was able to forward full details of the research and its findings. The researchers had created chemical compounds containing different allotropes than those found in nature. In animal testing, they found that some biochemical processes, particularly those involving enzymes, could be disrupted. The worst disruption occurred when a cis allotrope was substituted for a trans allotrope. Prancan wondered if the natural allotropes found in native biochemistry differed from those in Kastusians. Unfortunately, the laboratory on the spaceship was not equipped to provide the answer to that question.

As the years passed, the general situation deteriorated. One group of crossbreds took over an iron foundry and diverted its production into weapon making. One type of weapon was a three-foot-long narrow piece of iron with sharpened edges and a pointed end. Another was a long wooden shaft with a steel point affixed. This was thrown towards its target. The same group killed the crew of one of the craft who had arrived to enable a report to be made. The craft was then used to hunt down perceived opponents more efficiently.

That atrocity was surpassed a few years later. One settlement reported that an armed group had captured over two hundred mostly pure native people and taken them to work on land the group controlled. Slavery had been born.

Around one hundred and eighty years after the Kastusian landing, the crew of the spaceship numbered just three, one of whom was Jeflis. When they saw a group of armed men approaching, they retreated into the spaceship closing the doors, thinking they would be safe inside. The ship had not flown in many years, and it would take a couple of hours to bring all the necessary systems back into life. Concentrating on that task, they did not see their attackers piling wood and straw all around them. It was only when the temperature inside the ship increased dramatically that they realised they were doomed. Jeflis kept communicating with Maxtus until the end. It is not clear whether she or the equipment succumbed first.

For information on how events panned out between then and the Carnacan arrival almost 20,000 years later, one must rely on human records, which are rather sketchy especially in the earlier millennia.

I certainly needed that stiff drink. As I listened to Ixos, I felt stunned, yet, at the same time, excited. The knowledge that humanity is, to put it bluntly, a mongrel species was unsettling. But that knowledge was a starting point in understanding those aspects of human behaviour that had puzzled and concerned Carnac. It was certainly reassuring that humanity had once been a well ordered, peaceable species. Humanity could not be blamed for acceding to the requests made by the Kastusians regarding crossbreeding. That idea had originated on Kastus where medical science was immeasurably more advanced than on Earth. One also noted that Earth lost a great deal more than Kastus. Kastus lost the potential descendants of the evacuees. Earth lost many people down the ages as a result of conflicts that would not have occurred without the crossbreeding. It had also destroyed its social order.

My excitement came from the realisation that various tales, which were universally regarded as myths, were actually garbled descriptions of historical events. Greek legend spoke about gods on Mount Olympus. It now seemed that the Kastusians were those gods. Were those fiery chariots in the Old Testament Kastusian craft? The story of the Tower of Babel must be seen in a different light now that we know that 22,000 years ago, all humanity spoke the same language. Even that bit in the bible referring to the sons of god sleeping with the daughters of men now made sense. I recalled reading with great scepticism the writings of Von Daniken. Some of his ideas were still fanciful, but his basic premise, that people from another planet had visited Earth, had now turned out to be true.

I asked Ixos what Carnacan scientists thought was the cause of the severe deterioration in behaviour brought about by crossbreeding. It seemed they did not know. They had been able to test the theory that allotropic molecules were involved. Intensive study of the Kastusian archive allowed them to identify various allotropes involved in the biochemistry of that species. These were compared to the allotropes identified following the dissection of those humans who had been brought to Carnac. It had to be remembered that those humans were almost certainly all crossbreds. Even so, the absence of any differences between human allotropes and the Kastusian equivalent made it unlikely that the explanation lay with them. Investigations continued on Carnac. One school of thought was that genes somehow possessed an ability to recognise the presence of "alien" genes.

Until the question was answered, Carnac was proceeding on the assumption that any crossbreeding, whether with humanity or one of the other two species under observation, was likely to produce a similarly undesirable outcome. Accordingly, all three projects were being terminated. Should evidence emerge, at some stage in the future, to the contrary, the other two projects could be restarted.

Our long conversation concluded with a question from Ixos: "Would you like to leave with us?"

Chapter 11

Ixos agreed to my request for time to consider his question. It was not every day one was asked to consider permanent emigration from one's home planet. There was a lot to think about. I did not anticipate getting much sleep that night.

Initially, I simply could not decide which way I wanted to go. The prospect of becoming the first human to leave the solar system was exciting, indeed. The farthest any other person had travelled was to the NASA base on Mars, and only a dozen astronauts had been there. But did I want to sever all connection with the rest of humanity? Whilst all of the friends I had made when I first moved to Newry were long since dead, I had made many new friends. Once people got past my celebrity and came to know me, they treated me just like any other middle-aged man. I really was pulled both ways.

Eventually, as daytime approached and just as I was starting to doze off, the kernel of an idea began to form. Perhaps humanity could fare better this time round than it did when the Kastusians were here. My decision on whether to go or stay would depend on the responses I received to certain questions and requests.

When I next spoke to Ixos, instead of delivering my decision, I asked him whether the Carnacans intended to depart in secret or make a grand exit. He informed me that the current plan was to depart secretly as there was nothing to be gained by having the departure come to the attention of humanity. He listened intently as I outlined what I had in mind. When I finished, Ixos said he would need to consult Carnac regarding my proposal. However, he was able to fill me in on other aspects of the planned departure. All bases were being left intact. The stuff barrier should prevent their discovery by humans. Even if somebody did detect the barrier, human technology was not sufficiently advanced to enable it to be penetrated. If, by some unforeseen circumstance, the barrier was breached, Carnac thought humans would be unable to reverse engineer the stuff. But, following a precautionary principle, all time dilators were being taken back to Carnac.

A few hours later, Besil came to *Domhain Eile* to inform me that Ixos had asked that I go to Knocknashee as soon as possible. Instead of going down the steps into the base, Besil took me down to the fairy thorn where Ixos awaited. He showed me how to operate the sub-ethereal communicator before I found myself in conversation with Carnac. I was quizzed about why I was proposing a particular course of action and what I thought it would achieve. I explained my thinking as best I could and was informed that I would be told of Carnac's response as soon as possible. The response came a few hours later, and it was positive.

I hoped the departure timetable would allow me sufficient time to do all that I wanted to do before I left Earth. There were many friends to whom I wished to say farewell. I did not tell an out-right lie when I said I was emigrating, and it might be perma-nently. A couple of local restaurants benefitted greatly as I en-tertained groups of friends to farewell dinners. The waiting staff also had a bonanza as many of my guests left generous tips once they discovered I had picked up the tab.

I caused a certain amount of astonishment in my bank when I requested bank drafts in various large amounts made out in favour of a number of charities. The largest was in the amount of £250,000 in favour of Trocaire. Purchasing these drafts re-duced my bank balance to less than £1,000.

In other financial matters, I indulged my sense of mischief. I composed letters to each of the state pension authorities and the administrators of my civil service pension. I informed them that I was emigrating from N Ireland but would be maintaining the bank account into which the pension was paid. To the state pension people, I wrote that I was aware that the annual uprating did not apply to pensioners resident in certain countries but was unsure whether Carnac was one such place. I added that, as a minimum, I expected the pension to be paid at the current rate until my death. To the other pension administrators, I simply said that I had a legal entitlement to receive the indexed pension until I died. As I wrote the letters, my only regret was that I would not be around to receive the replies.

Bringing this chronicle up to date consumed quite a chunk of time. I continued working on it until the morning of the planned departure. To enable it to cover events right up to the moment of departure, I described the events on the day of departure as they had been planned to happen by Carnac and me. I printed one hard copy and also downloaded the document on to a memory stick. These I put into a package addressed to a firm of publishers. The covering letter began, "Yes! I am that Tony O'Gallagher." The letter also contained my instructions as to whom any royalties accruing to me were to be paid.

Another matter to which I attended was preparing a package to be sent to the World Bridge Federation. This would contain printouts of all the records of the only Antarctic bridge congress, including hand records and score sheets for all boards. I reckoned that, once published, these would be a source of envy and amazement to even the best human bridge players.

Another time-consuming matter was one that involved communications with scientists on Carnac. Initially, they had been surprised that I had any knowledge of the topic. I explained the circumstances in which I learned about it from Jamil. The scientists thought I could not have selected anything better for what I planned. I was pleased to discover that I could deal with the relevant government department online. I had feared I might need to travel to London.

The days seemed to fly by as departure date approached. With four days to go, I emailed Jake Jackson. Following his first interview with me, his career had blossomed and he rose to political editor with the BBC. He had retired a couple of years earlier, but he was still a respected figure in the media world. He was also a person I trusted. So, I asked him to meet me at Stonehenge at noon on 15 May 2136 where I would provide him with the greatest news story of all time. Naturally enough, Jake pressed me for more information, but I refused. I suggested he bring a good camera man with him.

The day before departure, I visited the family plot in St Patrick's cemetery in Armagh to place some flowers. I repeated the process in St Mary's cemetery in Newry where my grandmother and aunt had been buried. Finally, I visited a third grave, that of Billy McConkey. The card with those flowers bore the legend, "You never knew what you started."

As soon as the Post Office opened on the 15th, I handed in a parcel addressed to a publishing firm, another to the World Bridge Federation and a bundle of letters. Some of these were to different charities, others to a number of pharmaceutical companies, one to a firm of solicitors setting out my instructions regarding a piece of intellectual property and one to my bank giving instructions on future disbursements. This business completed, it was back to Knocknashee to await the arrival of the spaceship.

As we were waiting, Ixos explained that all of the recording devices would continue to function. The sub-ethereal communicator was programmed to transmit all of the recordings to Carnac on a regular basis. Over time, some recording devices would be discovered and thereby cease to be effective but sufficient would remain operational.

The trip to Stonehenge took less than half an hour, and we arrived at around five to twelve. Jake and his camera man were already there. As they chatted, Jake was scanning the approach road and checking his watch. At noon precisely, I exited the spaceship and said in a loud voice, "You are looking well, Jake." As he turned to face me, he asked, "Where did you come from, and what's this big story?" As I invited the pair to follow me, Tatos tweaked the stuff skin, and the spaceship became visible. Being the seasoned reporter that he was, Jake tried to keep his composure, but his astonishment was plain to see. I could not resist a naughty, "Don't worry. You will be safe with me," as we entered the ship.

It had been decided that the time dilator would be switched off whilst Jake and his camera man were on board. If it was on, the conversation with Jake would require several hours of terrestrial time during which those who had witnessed the spaceship appear could contact the authorities. Even though the terrestrial military would be incapable of damaging the spaceship, any such intervention would be unwelcome. Ixos and Besil were waiting in a small room. Through a clear partition, one could see the crews from Knocknashee, Carlow and two Scottish bases reclining on low couches. Jake started to fire a series of questions, but Ixos raised a hand to silence him. He informed him that he would make a brief statement which would be followed by one from me.

Ixos's statement was as follows. "My companions and I are from the planet Carnac. People from Carnac have lived on Earth for almost 3,000 years. During that time, we have observed human behaviour and watched the progression from a species with little scientific knowledge and only primitive technology to present-day humanity. While much more progress would be required to bring human science and technology anywhere close to that of Carnac, humanity should be proud of its achievements. But one aspect of human behaviour is of major concern to us. Many humans display much aggression and readily resort to violence. We have witnessed many conflicts and wars that have resulted in great loss of life and extensive destruction of buildings and infrastructure. Such behaviour is unknown on Carnac. Such behaviour is totally unacceptable. We know that one cannot change one's nature. But we also know that one can modify one's actions, control one's passions. One can learn to resist violent urges. We want to assist humanity but, for us to do so, humanity must learn to assist itself. Humans need to learn that conflict and war are never a benefit to anyone. If you think differently, then your head's a marley. Humans should also learn that the greatest progress occurs when food and other goods are shared more equitably. This is what we offer to humanity. We will continue to observe your behaviour. Should two hundred years elapse without any conflict, even a minor localised one, then Carnac will send some of its people to help humanity develop its scientific knowledge and technology and provide other technology currently beyond human imagination. As a gesture of goodwill, we are leaving a gift to humanity which Tony will describe. Once he has done so, we will depart. Whether people from Carnac ever return will depend on human behaviour. Clanwe yashpak!"

Before Jake could say anything, I launched into my statement. "As many will know, I am a hundred and eighty four years old. This morning, I have sent a book to a firm of publishers that will reveal the true reason for my longevity. It will also answer many of your questions about the Carnacan presence on Earth and why they are departing. Their gift to humanity is a chemical formula and details of the necessary raw ingredients and the manufacturing process. To ensure that the product will be universally available at a reasonable cost, I have taken out the necessary patents and instructed my solicitors to transfer these patents into the joint ownership of three organisations devoted to the rights and welfare of women. I have sent details of the formula and production method to several pharmaceutical companies along with a licence to produce the product, the licence being conditional on the product being made available at reasonable cost. A tablet containing ten milligrams of this product, if consumed once a week, will completely halt the menstrual cycle. Women will experience periods only if they wish to do so. The product provides contraception, which is one hundred per cent effective and there are no known side effects. On ceasing to take the product, the menstrual cycle returns to normal within a month. Future fertility is unaffected. I am leaving Earth with my Carnacan friends. I do not think I will ever return. Before I go, I would like to thank all who have given me their friendship or shown me kindness. Clanwe yashpak."

Jake was full of questions, but Ixos said departure time had arrived. As the camera man followed Jake out of the spaceship, I passed him an envelope containing the name and address of the publisher to whom I had sent my chronicle telling him that they would likely pay well for some of his photography. There would be plenty of mobile phone footage of the exterior of the spaceship, but he was the only one with footage of the interior and the Carnacans. I added that he should look up when he was on the ground.

As he and Jake looked skywards, the pilots tweaked the stuff skin so that simultaneously forty spaceships appeared overhead hovering around five hundred feet up. Five seconds later, another forty appeared, then another forty until three hundred and ninety nine were visible in the sky. I had known what was going to happen but still found it an amazing sight. Cecil B de Mille could not have staged it any better. So, what the occupants of the many cars that stopped on nearby roads made of it, I simply could not imagine.

Once all the Carnacan spaceships were visible, Tatos took off and we took our place in the fleet. Then, following another tweak, the human bystanders saw the entire fleet just vanish. It reappeared minutes later flying in formation over London before it vanished again. Next came Berlin, then Madrid, Moscow, Paris and Stockholm as it followed a seemingly erratic course over the planet's surface. That course was designed to make it impossible for anyone to predict where it would next appear. Not that it would have made any significant difference. The spaceships could easily outrun and outperform any human aircraft. The only missiles capable of inflicting damage were nuclear missiles, the use of which at low altitude would kill many more humans than Carnacans. The world tour finished directly over the United Nations headquarters in New York where the fleet effortlessly changed formation forming two concentric circles.

We headed for Carnac.

Epilogue

As we cruised away from Earth, we monitored political and media reaction to Jake's report and the appearance of the Carnacan fleet. There was a surprising degree of unanimity. One hundred and eighty countries submitted requests for a debate in the United Nations General Assembly during which a global treaty, drafted by Switzerland, would be considered. The debate took place, and the text of the treaty was approved unanimously. No country with a permanent seat on the Security Council wielded a veto. There occurred a grand ratification ceremony where every state on the planet, bar one, signed on the dotted line. Vatican City refused, citing a rather complex doctrinal objection. Whether all signatories would continue to comply with the terms of the treaty was yet to be seen.

Media attention remained intense for weeks. Every possible angle was covered, and all kinds of cranks were interviewed. There were those who maintained that the whole thing had been faked. One attention seeker declared that the Carnacan fleet had been an optical illusion created by himself. Some religious fanatics argued that the Carnacans were really angels seeking to persuade humanity to reform before the second coming. One delusional character claimed that Tony O'Gallagher had sat beside him in primary school from 2089 until 2096.

Initially, much of the English-speaking world was bemused by the words, "His head's a marley." Rather mischievously, Jake did not enlighten the various pundits who speculated on what they meant. People in Northern Ireland derived much amusement from this.

An attempt was made to prevent publication of my chronicle. In the UK, the government of the day was, by nature, very authoritarian. The remarks by Ixos had left ministers wondering just how much Carnac, and by extension, Tony O'Gallagher, knew about their deliberations and decisions on certain matters. Some of that information would be political dynamite and extremely damaging to their prospects of retaining power after the next election. They wished to gain control of the book in order that they might review its content and, if necessary, publish a redacted version. They issued an order to all publishers based in the UK prohibiting publication or distribution of the book and requiring all copies of any such manuscript or computer file to be delivered to the Home Office. The order also forbade the recipient from disclosing to any other person that it had been made. This effectively made it impossible to seek judicial review of the order. So draconian were such orders that the legislation provided they could be made only with the prior consent of the Supreme Court. Obtaining such consent took forty-eight hours, and that delay proved to be significant.

Jake's camera man had phoned my publisher just after the fleet disappeared. They had prior experience of government attempting to censor various publications and decided to put a copy of the chronicle beyond its reach. Immediately after my package arrived, an electronic copy was sent to their office in Dublin. They would have liked to publish it online, but my letter had made it absolutely clear that the chronicle was to be published in book form only. Even with working around the clock, that would still take a few days.

Not wanting to give the government any opportunity to publish online before the book came out, they encrypted the computer file they supplied to the Home Office. They then maintained that this was how the chronicle had been received by them. The encryption was very strong, and the book was published in Dublin amid great fanfare. Rather mischievously, the publishers placed full-page adverts in *The Irish Times* and *Irish Independent*, both of which were available in the UK. They showed Besil and me standing side by side. In the original photograph, we had been holding a bridge trophy. The photoshopped version had us holding a copy of the book and both of us sported gags. The legend read: "Gagged in the UK."

The public reaction was one of universal fury. Within thirty-six hours, an online petition had attracted more than 35 million signatures. Sensing political annihilation, and discovering that their fears had been groundless, the government rescinded the orders prohibiting publication.

Within three weeks, translations into French, German, and Mandarin were published. Spanish, Japanese, Russian, Arabic, Italian, and Bengali soon followed, and by the end of the year, it was available in every language. Total sales worldwide exceeded 800 million copies.

Following publication of the book, extensive searches were initiated to try and locate the Carnacan bases. Straightened metal coat hangers became something of a fashion accessory even though few people could actually use them. The barrier at Knocknashee was found very quickly, but efforts to breach it proved unsuccessful. The same situation prevailed at the forty-two other bases identified.

Many recording devices were located but, as Ixos pointed out, this did not matter. The humanity project was over so no new observations were needed. Human media would continue to be monitored to enable Carnac to decide on whether humanity would receive technological assistance.

I celebrated my two hundredth birthday in deep space. To my pleasure and surprise, Besil produced a couple of bottles of champagne apparently purchased during a late night trip to Tesco in Newry shortly before departure. Her rendition of "Happy Birthday" was something else.

The author

Tony O'Gallagher has led a relatively quiet life in Newry, Northern Ireland. He was born in the early 1950s in London and attended a Christian Brothers' grammar school. He is divorced and has three sons. His hobbies include playing bridge, reading and Sudoku, as well as divining water. He had held some high-ranking positions within the Northern Ireland Bridge Union and the Irish Bridge Union. This book, Clanwe Yashpack, is his first published work.